ARIANA

The Making of a Queen

A Novel

Rachel Ann Nunes

Covenant Communications, Inc.

Published by Covenant Communications, Inc.
American Fork, Utah

Printed in the United States of America
First Printing: September 1996

01 00   10 9 8 7 6 5

ISBN 1-57734-025-6

Dedication

To my mother, who taught me to read when I was four, instilling in me a lifetime passion for words.

And to my father, who tried to teach me proper grammar, and who gave me a love of foreign places and people.

CHAPTER ONE

Warm rain fell softly in the dark Parisian night, yet strongly enough to mingle with the tears that fell down my face, masking them completely as I stood against the balcony railing in the cheap hotel. Not that there was anyone around to see that I was crying, or to care about my pain. It should have been one of the happiest days in any woman's life—full of wonder, discovery, and love. But on this night, my first since becoming a wife earlier that day, I was alone and crying.

My new husband, Jacques, was out drinking with his friends, celebrating our marriage in the way he knew best, and shattering my dreams—dreams that had already been thin enough to begin with. Still, I guessed I was lucky he had gone through with the wedding in the first place. One thing I did know was that I loved him with a first love's passion, even though he had left me alone on this of all nights.

Noise blared from the next-door window—another American song idolized for its irreverence and suggestiveness, a typical theme of the nineties. Ordinarily, I would appreciate the music; but tonight it only intensified my loneliness.

The rain came down faster now, and I could see figures scurrying to the underground metro where it was dry. The hole seemed to swallow the people as they ran down its stairs, their heads bowed and bodies huddled against the rain. It was summer; the tourist season was upon Paris, and the weekend crowds seemed undiminished even by the late hour and the rain. Along the road I could see the bars, lighted and beckoning. I wondered idly which of them held my new husband, and a fresh batch of not-so-quiet sobs erupted at the thought.

If only Antoine were alive! The thought came suddenly but not so unexpectedly. The rain would always remind me of Antoine and how he had been ripped from my life, my world changed forever. I would never forget how, up until nine months ago, Antoine had been my world. He had always taken care of me.

"Come on, let's go do something!" Antoine would shout at me whenever I was depressed. "There's no use in hanging around feeling sorry for ourselves!" Then he'd grin at me and I couldn't help but smile back. I'd put my hand trustingly in his, willing to go anywhere with the brother I adored, knowing that with him my problems would disappear.

My brother had been loved by everybody who knew him. He had the sort of face even strangers felt attracted to and trusted. He always kept their trust and mine—except that once, when he died and left me all alone. But I really couldn't fault him for that; he would never have left me on purpose.

"Where are you children off to today?" Father beamed down on us that last day we spent together. He laid a proud hand on Antoine's shoulder. "You will take care of Ariana, won't you?"

Antoine, seeing my frustration at his words, replied, "She's hardly a baby, Father. But I will look after her, and she after me, as we always have." That made me feel better, since we were the same age—the only difference being that he had been born a boy and I a girl. Of course, with the French double standard, that alone was enough. Though we would soon be entering the twenty-first century, my old-fashioned father believed boys were somehow more competent in all areas of life than their helpless female counterparts.

"What time will you be home?" my mother asked.

"I don't know," Antoine said offhandedly. "Sometime before dark, I assume." He flashed her his smile before she could object, melting her instantly as usual.

Oh, I didn't mind that my parents loved Antoine so. I did, too. In my eyes, as in theirs, he did no wrong. He always included me in everything he chose to do, giving me the freedom I would never have known otherwise. He never made me feel I was just something extra that had happened when my parents had tried to have the baby boy they had longed for, though that was the truth.

Together we spent many days roaming Paris where we lived, using the metro to take our explorations further, until I felt I knew Paris and the surrounding area better than I knew my own bedroom. Yes, I had many good memories of Antoine. I had especially loved walking along the Seine River, where numerous artists and others set up to sell their talents and various pieces of junk they called "souvenirs" to the many tourists. It was fun being near people who were so different from me, yet somehow the same. I adored watching and studying them, particularly when they weren't aware of me.

"It's getting late," Antoine had said to me that last day in September, now nine months past. He glanced at his watch. We had been walking near the river at the end of our adventure-filled day of roaming the catacombs in several of the nearby cathedrals. "We just have time to get home before dinner. Mother will be expecting us." I wanted to protest, but he was right. Mother would be expecting us, and Antoine was a good son to remember that. He was always good to everyone. Seeing my understanding, he smiled, making me glad I had not objected.

We took the metro home that night, and for some reason the train stopped between stations. The lights went off and we were alone in the dark. Worry crept up inside of me; I had never felt comfortable in dark, closed-in spaces. "Don't worry," Antoine said, ever aware of my feelings in the way that close twins were. "They'll come back on soon."

As if to obey him, the lights flickered on. But still the train did not move. I tried to peer out into the dark tunnel, but could see only my worried expression reflected in the glass.

"Look at this!" Antoine shouted. He had hold of two of the bars that were meant to steady standing passengers at rush hour, and he was hanging upside down on them like a monkey.

"Are you crazy, Antoine?" I exclaimed. We were alone in the car, but people from the next car could see him if they glanced though windows in the connecting doors.

"Come on!" he cried, doing a flip and swinging further down the bars.

"We're not ten anymore, Antoine!" I protested, remembering the time when we had perfected our antics on similar bars. But that had been over seven years ago—we were nearly adults now. In six months we would be eighteen.

"Oh, Ari!" Antoine tossed his dark head around to gaze at me, his deep brown eyes dancing. Then he uttered the prophetic words that would echo in my mind forever: "We're only seventeen, we're not dead and buried yet!" At that I had to join him, my fear of the stopped train vanishing completely. Of course, looking back, I know that to comfort me was the only reason he had hung on the bars that night. He had always taken care of me.

Pain ripped through my soul as it always did at this point in the memories, for the train incident had happened the night before he died. Now I clutched tightly at the balcony railing until my hands turned white and began to ache. The light from the hotel room came through the tiny glass door, its feeble rays barely reaching me in the dark. Dressed in my thin, dark-blue nightgown, I felt suddenly cold. But still I lingered at the railing where the rain could reach me, almost wishing it could wash me away—or at least wash away the feelings that tortured my heart.

"Oh, Antoine," I whispered into the night. "If only you hadn't left, then things would not be so mixed up." But he was gone forever, and anything I said to him wouldn't make any difference. Antoine existed no more, except in my memories.

I continued to stare out into the night, but I didn't see the streets or the cobblestone sidewalks—only the frozen expression on my father's face the day Antoine died. It had been raining all morning long, turning from a soft pitter-patter to an earnest downpour. Antoine had already left for his early class at the private school we attended. Unlike me, he never passed up a chance for the early classes. He rode the metro, as we all did; it was the fastest way to get anywhere in Paris because you didn't have to worry about finding a parking place.

My parents and I were finishing up our croissants and coffee at the table when the phone rang shrilly into the silence; there was always a lot of silence when Antoine was absent. My father got up and reached for the phone. "Hello?" he said in his decisive voice.

Then, "Yes, this is he."

As the person on the other end of the phone continued, my father's face grew stark white, contrasting sharply with his dark hair and moustache. "No! No! It can't be true!" he exclaimed suddenly and painfully, but his voice sounded defeated. He listened further before asking shakily, "When did it happen?" And then, "What time should I come down? Okay. Thanks for calling."

When he turned to us, he was no longer the man I thought I knew. "Antoine is dead," he said dully. "A car hit him on his way to school."

"Oh, no!" my mother gasped and began to cry. "What happened?"

"He's dead, it's over!" my father spoke harshly. The pain in his eyes was too terrible for me to bear. "What does it matter how?"

The reality that Antoine was never coming back hit me like the weight of an anchor, and my anguished words exploded into the air. "Oh, please, not Antoine! Oh, why did it have to be Antoine?"

My parents turned slowly to face me, seeming almost surprised at my presence. I thought for a minute they would reach out to me, that we could turn to each other in our shared grief. But they didn't. My father turned abruptly on his heel and went into his office, shutting the door firmly behind him. My mother stared after him for a long moment, the hurt evident on her face, then she also turned and ran down the hall to her room, her loud sobs filling the sudden silence.

"Oh, Antoine," I whispered. "We are lost without you!"

I stood in the dining room alone, not knowing what to do. I lifted my eyes to the large mirror on the wall opposite me. There I could see my face, still tan from summer, with my short, dark hair and large brown eyes—each feature a feminine version of Antoine's. No wonder my parents couldn't bear to look at me!

For a very brief instant, I saw my brother's face instead of mine in the mirror. I could almost hear him speak the words he'd said on the train the night before: "Oh, Ari! We're only seventeen, we're not dead and buried yet!" I gasped and ran to the mirror, but he was gone and I was truly alone. My face was now white beneath my tan, but I didn't cry. I bit my lip until the blood came, but I still didn't cry. Not then.

I didn't know it at the time, but my parents' reactions that day were to develop into a more permanent reality. My father spent more time at work, and I often went days without catching so much as a glimpse of him. When I did see him, he was cold and withdrawn, the light gone from his eyes. Mother was worse, sinking into a shell of her own making. She talked to me but seemed to see right through me, her face a bitter mask of pain and loss. I spent less and less time at home, but it seemed my absence went unnoticed. I knew they would never love me as they had Antoine, that I could never replace him in their hearts. And I began to hate them for it.

The day of Antoine's funeral, it had finally stopped raining. The sun shone brightly down on the mourners, but its warmth did not reach our hearts. I stood dutifully by my parents during the short graveside service and while they lowered the coffin into the hole that seemed to ravage the earth. But I fled from the cemetery as they began to throw the dirt on the coffin. I couldn't bear to see them do that to Antoine; it was too final. At that moment I knew my life was over; how could I possible live without my other half?

I ended up at my favorite section of the Seine where we had spent so much time, Antoine and I. Breathless and sweating when I arrived, I lifted my face to gaze out over the water, hoping for a breeze and maybe some kind of comfort. There was neither—only boats, faceless people, and squawking seagulls.

I walked blindly and aimlessly for a while. Suddenly I stopped and stared, surprised to see a group of young men with short hair and suits, singing in the street. Several young woman were among them, holding up a big sign proclaiming "Families Are Forever!"

What a bunch of idiots! I thought. *Nothing is forever.* I had learned that lesson only too well.

Other young men and women with the singers were stopping people passing nearby and talking with them. One of the men—a boy, really—with a shock of bright red hair approached me with a pamphlet. His accent betrayed that he was a foreigner, probably from America by the sound. "Here," he said, thrusting the little booklet into my hand. "Did you know that families can be together forever?" His voice was sincere, his eyes clear; I knew he believed what he was saying, but in my grief-induced haze, I didn't care.

I stopped in my tracks, whirling on him, my eyes flashing. "You don't know what you're talking about!" I said angrily, looking up into his blue eyes. "Has anyone you loved more than life itself ever died? Someone who was so much a part of you that you'd rather die than live without him?" The tall boy shook his head and opened his mouth to speak, but I continued quickly. "Well, I know how it feels, and anything you can make up won't change the fact that my brother is dead and gone from me forever!"

I crumpled the thin pamphlet in front of his face and threw it to the ground. Then I added cruelly, "Now get out of my way and leave me alone!" The young man stepped back and I glanced up at him. I had expected to find hurt and anger in those clear eyes, but all I saw was pity and, strangely, love. It made me even more furious that the only one who seemed to show me what I so desperately needed was a red-haired stranger from another country.

"I am sorry," the young man said softly and hesitantly in his uncertain French. "I hope you find what you need. I will pray for you."

How dare he! I thought, and was about to say something even more unkind, but he was already gone, leaving me alone as I had requested. I went home and cried as I hadn't been able to since Antoine's death earlier in the week—red-hot tears that seemed to sear my cheeks as they fell. There seemed to be no end to the bitter flood. My throat felt raw and my eyes were swollen, but the ache in my heart was worse. I thought I was going to die, even hoped that I would.

At last the torrent subsided, and through my abating tears I spied my parents' liquor cabinet. I had never been drunk before, but I often had alcohol with dinner. I knew it would give me a euphoria that would make me temporarily forget. I began to drink, and an unnatural warmth flooded through me.

Yet I didn't forget, not even for a moment, and all my drunkenness did was to put another wedge between me and my parents when they came home to find me nearly passed out. They utterly forbade me to drink. I didn't give it up, though; I continued drinking at home or with friends in the months that followed. My parents' anger was better than their indifference.

A loud knocking at the hotel door brought me abruptly back to the present. I came in from the balcony, hardly noticing my wet hair and the thin nightgown clinging to my body. I glanced at the TV which I had left on. The sound was muted, but I could see the latest Disney cartoon movie filling the screen, complete with French subtitles. The movie was playing on one of the special TV channels—the only modern concession the run-down hotel had made for its questionable clientele. I had always enjoyed Disney movies—one more thing I had shared with Antoine—but this time I didn't stop to watch.

The knocking sounded again. Could it be Jacques? And it was only one o'clock in the morning! With a hopeful heart, I hurried to the door and threw it open to reveal not Jacques but Paulette, the girl who had become my best friend after Antoine's death.

The light went out of my eyes. "Oh, hi, Paulette." I stood back and let her enter the room. As she swept past me I could smell the cigarette smoke in her hair and the alcohol on her breath. Involuntarily, I flinched. In the months after Antoine's death, those things had been my constant companions—but no more. I had someone else to think of now.

When I had shut the door, she turned her plain face to me. "Ariana, you're soaking wet! Haven't you got any sense? I—" She broke off when she saw the pain in my face. "Oh, I'm sorry, Ariana, I know you wanted Jacques, but he's not coming. I was just down at the bar and saw him and the gang. That's why I came. I knew that you were alone and thought you could use some company. Come on." She put her arm around my shoulders. "Let's get you out of these wet things." Numbly, I let her lead me to the bathroom.

A short time later we sat together on the large bed. I was now wearing a long t-shirt and my robe instead of the negligee. I drew my feet onto the bed and lay back on a mound I had made of the pillows, my fingers plucking carelessly at the faded green blanket, worn but clean. Paulette drew out a thin, homemade cigarette and lit up, breathing deeply. She offered it to me, but I refused as I hadn't in the weeks and months following Antoine's funeral.

Antoine had never liked Paulette, who lived nearby, though she would have given anything to date him. "I don't think you should hang around with her," he had told me. So I hadn't; I was too busy with school and spending time with him, anyway. Then he died, and suddenly I didn't care about things anymore. I stopped going to school and began to hang out with Paulette, who hadn't been to school for years.

"It's too bad about your brother, Ari," she had said the first day she found me drinking alone in the park. That had been the day after Antoine's funeral.

"Ariana," I said dully. "Don't call me Ari ever again." In my eyes, Ari had died with Antoine.

"He was one good-looking guy. He . . ." Paulette had talked on, but I hadn't really heard her; it was just nice to have someone to sit with. She pulled out some of her thin cigarettes. "Want one?"

For the first time I looked into her clouded eyes. "What is it?"

"Marijuana. It will help you feel better."

I took the cigarette and breathed in, hesitantly at first and then more deeply, coughing some but at last finding some relief for the aching pain in my heart. I didn't realize at the time that drugs would bring much more misery to my life than I could ever imagine.

After that day at the park, Paulette and I became inseparable. We hung out with a group of teenagers like us, brave on the outside, yet each hurting in some way on the inside. We drank all the time, went dancing, and smoked. Sometimes I never even bothered to go home. At times my parents didn't notice, at others they yelled at me, but it made no difference. I was living my own life.

Then I met Jacques. I had just turned eighteen, and we were at our favorite dance club celebrating when I saw a good-looking young man with dark-blond hair come from across the room toward our group. Several of the guys got up to meet him.

"Hey, welcome back, Jacques! How did things go on the Riviera?"

"Good, good," Jacques replied, a sincere smile on his handsome face. "But I missed you all." His eyes suddenly spotted me. "Who's this? Someone new to our little group?"

"I'm Ariana," I said with a smile. "It's my birthday, and we're celebrating."

Jacques came to sit beside me and put a casual arm around the back of my chair. "I'm glad to meet you, Ariana." His brown eyes burned into my own. "Very glad."

"Oh, yeah, I'm sure you are," I joked dryly. "I've heard all about you, Jacques, and your way with women."

He smiled impudently. "Good, then you will let me help you have a great birthday, won't you? I'll make it one you'll never forget!"

And he did. We danced together all night, laughing and joking. He was so handsome and attentive, always saying just the right thing. He knew how to treat a woman, how to flatter her and make her feel loved and cared for.

I didn't go home at all that night, not wanting to be separated from the dashing Jacques. The magic between us was strong, yet I feared it would vanish if we were parted, even for a few hours. The group of us crashed at someone's apartment, and we stayed up all night watching videos, smoking pot, and drinking. At last I went to sleep in the crook of Jacques' arm, feeling more content than I had since Antoine's death.

Jacques and I became a couple. The group seemed amazed that the wild Jacques had finally settled down, and I secretly worried that he would leave me. I didn't understand what he saw in me, a woman who had been rejected by her own parents. But he seemed genuinely fascinated and wanted to be a part of every aspect of my life—including my parents. I took Jacques to meet them a few days later, but they refused to accept him and even forbade me to see him. So less than a week after we met, I moved to Paulette's so that Jacques and I could spend every minute together. How could I have known I was only getting into more trouble? I had still been so innocent, even then. That had been just three months ago.

And now we were married, a thing we had decided to do only two days earlier—or rather, something I had convinced Jacques to do. When he finally agreed, Paulette and I had thrown together whatever kind of a ceremony and party we could. It wasn't much, but our friends pitched in to see that it had a least a semblance of a real wedding. My parents hadn't bothered to show up. They simply sent a substantial check, like some kind of a payoff. I wanted to rip it up into a hundred little pieces and send it back to them, but I had learned the importance of money in the last three months and knew that I would probably need it. I took the check immediately to the bank my father owned and operated, careful to choose a time when he wouldn't be there. I cashed the check, withdrew my own childhood savings, and took the money to another bank, where I opened an account that I kept secret even from Jacques. I wanted to save it for an emergency and couldn't trust him to do so; he seemed to live only for the moment.

"Ariana!" Paulette's voice was insistent. "Are you okay?"

I looked up at her, shaking away the memories. "Yes, I was just thinking."

"About Jacques?"

"Yes." I stared out the open balcony door and into the wet night and added softly, "And about Antoine." It was the first time I had said my brother's name to anyone since the day he died, and Paulette seemed taken aback.

"I'm sorry, Ariana. I know things haven't been easy for you. But now that you and Jacques are married, things will get better; you'll see. He's got a job now, and you can get one." Paulette's homely face was serious for once. The curious light of the room made her brown hair seem dull and lifeless, matching the look in her drugged eyes.

I smiled gently at her. "Yes, it just has to be okay." We hugged each other impulsively. Then I brought my hand to rest on my slightly swollen stomach, where my true hope for the future lay. There the baby I had conceived nearly three months ago, a week after meeting Jacques, was already making its welcome presence felt. For this baby, I had given up drinking and drugs. I was determined to do right by this life inside me, no matter what.

CHAPTER TWO

When Jacques came home three hours later, I was long asleep. I felt him slip into the big bed next to me, and his movements woke me. Sighing contentedly, I rolled over to him; but he was snoring almost before he hit the bed. Once again the tears came, and I blinked them back angrily. After all, he had at least come back to me.

For long moments I stared into the darkness, hearing Jacques' even breathing, yet feeling utterly alone. The night was finally still, broken only by an occasional shout or a lone car. The rain had stopped sometime while I had been sleeping, and I was fiercely glad. Now things would be all right again.

Almost unconsciously, my hand went to where my baby was growing. Sleep finally came, giving me a welcome relief from my lonely thoughts.

"Wake up, my love!" Jacques sang to me the next morning, kissing my face all over. He threw back the covers, and his hand slid down to my stomach. "Hey there, baby, wake up, Daddy wants to talk to you!" He made a show of kissing my belly noisily.

I opened one eye, then the other, and held out my arms for him. The dashing man I had fallen in love with was back!

He lay next to me, our arms entwined. "I've brought you breakfast," he whispered, kissing my ear. "Though we've slept so late it's more like lunch!" One brown eye closed in a wink.

I smiled and sat up slowly so I wouldn't feel nauseous; I still had morning sickness most days. While I ate, I examined Jacques carefully. His handsome face showed no signs of a hangover, though his eyes were still clouded with drugs.

"So what are we going to do today?" I asked, trying not to sound too hopeful.

He raised his eyebrows a couple of times suggestively, making me laugh. Then he said seriously, "Well, I thought we could find an apartment. I've got a few leads to follow up. I've had everyone I know out looking since we decided to get married. It has to be something we can afford."

I knew that meant a dump, but I didn't care; at least we would be together. I smiled. "At least we'll be able to pay for the first month's rent." I was referring to the paycheck Jacques had received just the day before our marriage.

His smile suddenly vanished. He pushed his longish hair back with a nervous hand. "I, uh, spent some of the money last night," he said hesitantly.

I wanted to scream at him but I didn't. More than anything, I wanted to keep the peace. Besides, getting upset would only make my morning sickness worse. "How much?"

He told me, and it wasn't as bad as I suspected. We would still be able to get the apartment, we just wouldn't be able to eat for more than a few days. But I knew we would manage somehow. At least he had a job, and I would look for work tomorrow.

After breakfast and a quick shower, we left the hotel. Outside, the June day was hot and sweltering, and many times I felt dizzy. Heat always seemed to do that to me since I became pregnant. But I was determined to spend as few days at the hotel as possible. We went from one old apartment building to the next, and just as I was giving up we found an apartment. It was a real dump, but at least it was a place to put our few belongings. Of course, the real selling point was that it was available immediately.

We paid the landlord and took a second look at the apartment. The paint was peeling and the room lacked air conditioning. The bathroom was so small that I couldn't go in without leaving the door open or I would feel claustrophobic. The vinyl tile in both the kitchen and bathroom was loose and coming up, the grayish carpet in the living room had dark stains everywhere, and the bedroom had no carpet at all, just heavily pocked and scratched hardwood flooring. I was suddenly glad my parents wouldn't be coming to see me in such a place, far removed from their elegant apartment on the better side of town.

We checked out of the hotel immediately. Paulette helped me move my few belongings from her parents' apartment, and one of the guys helped Jacques move his things from his cousin's where he'd been staying. There wasn't much to move, but the gang had found an old bed, a worn couch, and even a small table for us.

After helping us settle in, our friends laughed, making jokes about newlyweds, and left us to our honeymoon. But Jacques and I spent the day cleaning, or at least I did. Near dinner time, Jacques kissed me and went to get something for us to eat. He didn't come back until after eleven. By that time the apartment was liveable, though not completely clean.

I heard Jacques come in, and I glanced up at him tiredly from the kitchen floor where I was finishing up. "There must have been a long line," I said dryly, eyeing the plastic bag he held in his hands.

He grinned the beautiful smile that always made my heart skip a beat. "I got waylaid down by the bar, but I'm back now." He leaned down to kiss my cheek and handed me the sack. I grabbed it eagerly; I had eaten only bread since lunch and was feeling sick from the lack of good food. But all the bag held was wine, some pastries, and a few thin marijuana cigarettes.

I shook my head at him in anger. I knew that if I didn't eat soon, I would be very sick. "Jacques, I can't eat this junk! You heard what the doctor said when we went last week. I'm supposed to eat *healthy* stuff!"

But Jacques only smiled. He walked to the door and picked up another sack that he had left outside. "I know, gorgeous. That's why I brought you this." He handed me another sack full of yogurt, fruits, cheese, and various other healthy items I had asked him to buy. The food was still cold, so he must have just gotten it down at the new American-owned market on the corner that was open all night. "I must have mixed up the sacks," he continued as I tore off the lid on one of the drinkable yogurts.

I drank the yogurt before I replied, needing to stave off the nausea I was feeling. "Thanks, Jacques." I smiled and pulled my husband down to the floor to kiss him with all the passion of a young wife. He loved me so much. It would mean a lot of work and adjusting, but together we would make everything turn out right.

Morning dawned all too soon, bright, hot, and bustling. Jacques left early to go back to his job at a distribution warehouse, where he loaded boxes of clothing and other items into trucks all day. After kissing him goodbye I went back to bed, feeling sick from the late night before. But the sounds from the street and the heat that seeped in from the thin windows and poorly insulated walls made me even more ill. I got up and ate more of the food Jacques had brought me last night. I also spied the wine and marijuana on the counter; but, with a hand on my belly, I resisted the impulse. I was going to do right by my baby.

After breakfast, I showered and left the apartment to look for a job. Though still hot, the streets were better than the apartment because of a cool breeze that blew fresh air into my face. I set my jaw determinedly and started out. I tried nearly every supermarket and cafe in the area—it was the only work I was qualified for—with not even a hint of an offer. Half of the owners turned me away the minute they found out that I was expecting, so I soon started lying about my condition. I didn't feel good about it, but I needed to eat, didn't I?

The June sun was hot on my head and back as I reluctantly started searching the bars for openings. Not even a breeze broke the afternoon heat. I didn't like the idea of working in a bar, not appreciating the environment for my unborn child because of the smoke and the rough handling of the customers, but I felt I had no choice. Several of the workers told me there were openings, and asked me to come back the next day or later in the evening to talk to the managers. I saw a glimmer of hope, but was depressed nonetheless; I didn't want to work in a bar.

On the next street, I saw two young men in white shirts and short haircuts walking toward me. With a flash, I remembered the young American with the bright-red hair who had talked to me the day of Antoine's funeral nine months before. Pain washed over me, and I hurried across the street to avoid them.

"And he said he'd pray for me," I muttered. "Then why doesn't his God get me a decent job?" Of course, I wouldn't pray for myself; I didn't believe in a God that would let Antoine die. Besides, I had done well enough for myself, hadn't I? I had a husband and a baby—what more did I need? Certainly nothing that confused young man could have offered.

I shrugged the thoughts aside and hurried down the street to the next bar, and the next. I had no luck at either. I was only two streets away from our apartment when I suddenly saw a little cafe squeezed in between a shoe store and a cheap clothing outlet. Above the shop, as above many shops in Paris, loomed a three-story apartment building that appeared old but well-maintained.

I sighed, almost unwilling to risk rejection again. But something urged me over to the cafe. "Now would be a good time for you to pray," I murmured to the absent red-haired American boy. Again thoughts of Antoine flooded my mind, but I shoved them away. He was dead and gone forever; he couldn't help me now.

The shop had obviously just gotten over the last of the lunch crowd, for it was nearly empty. I arranged my blouse carefully over my slightly rounded stomach, though it was really not noticeable to those who didn't know how thin I had become since Antoine's death. Still, I felt as if a neon sign pointed to the baby inside of me.

The stout woman at the counter glanced up as I entered. One hand went up to push back a piece of gray hair that had escaped from her bun. She smiled wearily. "What would you like?"

Looking down at the splendid array of sandwiches and pastries, I felt suddenly hungry. I had stopped several times during the day to nibble at the cheese and bread I carried in my purse, but it was long past time for me to eat again. Nausea rose up in my throat, and I fought it down.

"I'm—I'm looking for work," I said as clearly as possible. "Do you have any openings?"

The lady studied me closely. "I don't hire people on drugs," she said severely.

"But I'm not," I protested uselessly as the room around me began to spin. I felt the blackness coming as it always did if I didn't eat at least every three hours, and suddenly I knew I was going to either be sick or pass out.

I turned from the woman as quickly as I could, hoping to at least make it out the door. The room whirled faster, and the blackness ate at the edges of my consciousness. Desperately, I clutched at the nearest table to try to steady myself. Then everything went black.

The next thing I knew, someone was dabbing my face with a cool cloth. "Wake up," said a woman's voice. It was the woman from the counter, but this time her voice was softer.

I sat up quickly, only to feel a return of the sickness. I lay back down on the cot and looked around the small room anxiously for my purse.

"My purse," I whispered urgently. "Where is it?"

The woman pursed her lips tightly, but handed me the purse. She obviously thought that I was going to pull out some drugs. I ignored her as I fumbled through my bag, my fingers eagerly closing around my one remaining cheese sandwich. I took a big bite and began to chew while the lady watched me curiously, a puzzled expression replacing her former disgust. After swallowing the first bite, I forced myself to eat more slowly; it would make my embarrassment even worse to throw up now.

After the small sandwich was gone, I looked up to see the woman still staring at me. I brought one hand instinctively to my stomach that jutted out, still small, but tellingly from my thin body as I lay on the cot. The woman saw the gesture, and her eyebrows raised slightly.

A bell rang in the distance, and the woman spoke. "I've got customers. You rest right here a moment and I'll be back." She smiled ever so briefly and disappeared through the door.

I sat up slowly and looked around the small, windowless room. A desk, a chair, the cot, and a large bookcase took up most of the space, obviously the woman's—or someone else's—office. I stood up and walked to the office door, which led into a large kitchen. Through a door beyond that I could see the stout woman helping a man at the counter.

There seemed to be no way out of the shop without passing the woman—unless one of the closed doors in the kitchen was a hall leading to her living quarters and perhaps a back door. It was likely, but I didn't want to make the situation worse by being caught snooping. I went back and sat down on the cot.

The woman returned in minutes. In her hands she carried a glass of milk. "Here, drink this," she said gruffly, handing it to me. "You should drink a lot of milk for the baby."

I took the milk and did as she asked. "I'm sorry," I said between sips. "I didn't realize I had gone so long without eating. I've been searching for a job all morning, and I was almost home when I saw your shop. I thought it couldn't hurt to try." I looked down at the floor and frowned. Whatever hope I had of getting a job at this particular cafe was long gone.

"What's your name?"

"Ariana. Ariana Merson, I mean Ariana de Cotte—I just got married recently."

"I'm Marguerite Geoffrin," the woman said. "My husband and I own this cafe and the apartment building over it. That's where he is right now, fixing a shower in one of the apartments while we're not too busy." She paused and her next words surprised me. "Business is very good, and in fact we do need someone to work the lunch and dinner shifts, Tuesday through Saturday. If you are willing to work, we'll give you a chance."

I looked up at her quickly, hardly daring to believe my luck. "But why?" The words came out before I had a chance to stop them. "What about when the baby comes?"

Marguerite smiled. "We'll cross that bridge when we come to it, Ariana. First let's see if you're a good worker."

I returned her smile. "Oh, I will be, I promise!" I exclaimed eagerly.

Marguerite held up her hand. "But there is one condition." Her expression was suddenly serious. "You will not use drugs of any kind."

I nodded. "I smoked pot for a few months," I confessed hesitantly. "But since I found out about the baby, I quit. I want to do what's right for it."

"Then it is agreed. You will earn the minimum salary plus two meals daily—or four half meals if you prefer, given your condition.

Be here tomorrow at noon. I think that you already have been too long on your feet today."

"Oh, thank you, Mrs. Geoffrin! And I won't let you down, I promise!"

"I hope not, Ariana," she said softly. Her eyes grew very sad. There was something more she wasn't telling me, some reason why she was giving me a chance, but I didn't want to push her. There would be time to find out her secrets soon enough.

Jacques and I celebrated that night, using our last money to pay for a cheap dinner at a restaurant, saving just enough to buy bread until payday. Since Jacques also ate a meal at work, we would survive. After dinner, he drank a lot of wine, but I was used to it. It made me happy to see my handsome husband enjoying himself.

The next weeks went by happily for me. The work at the cafe was strenuous, but the customers were nice, and I had plenty of opportunities to rest my feet when business wasn't so brisk. Marguerite, as I soon began to call Mrs. Geoffrin, even brought a tall stool to put behind the counter where I could sit and take the customers' money while she filled their orders during the rushes. Together, we developed a system which efficiently took care of customers in the minimum amount of time, and this only increased our business. In the kitchen her husband, Jules, was busy preparing the foods we served to the many customers. I felt more needed than I had ever felt in my life, even when Antoine lived. He had never needed me, only loved me.

Marguerite mothered me, and I responded happily. She filled a void in my life that I hadn't realized even existed. She and Jules became my closest friends besides Jacques and Paulette.

Summer turned into mid-October, and I blossomed—in more ways than one. Of course my stomach grew, and in fact I gained much-needed weight all over. But I also became more sure of myself and more positive of my future. The only strain on my new happiness was Jacques. Two months before the baby was due, four months after our marriage, he came home in a rage.

"I quit!" he exclaimed as he walked through the door. It was nearly noon, and I was getting ready to leave for my own job.

"You *what?*" I asked in amazement. He had been doing well at work, and together our wages were paying nicely for our expenses. We had bought a few new things for the apartment and for the baby, and I was already dreaming about moving to a better place— somewhere where the plumbing didn't need to be repaired, where there were no cockroaches, and where the neighbors didn't party all night long. Of course, we were as bad as our neighbors in the partying respect. Many nights our friends were over very late, watching our second-hand TV and smoking pot or drinking. I didn't mind it much as long as they stayed out of my room and didn't make us pay for the liquor. But still, things would have to change once the baby was born. I wanted my child to *be* something, not grow up to be a junkie.

"I quit my job," Jacques repeated. "They accused me of being on heroin, and I won't be treated badly for it."

I didn't say anything for a time, my suspicion growing by the minute. He hadn't exactly denied that he had taken the drug. "Well, are you?" I finally asked.

He glared at me. "It's none of their business what I do in my off time. It isn't affecting my work any."

I felt my heart racing. Marijuana was one thing, but heroin was something quite different. I had been in the gang long enough to see what kinds of lives were led by those who were addicted.

"It's no big deal," Jacques said, understanding immediately my expression of horror. "Everyone in the gang has been trying it lately, even Paulette."

"When?" I still couldn't believe it.

He shrugged. "While you're at work in the evenings. Sometimes here, sometimes at one of the others' apartments. What difference does it make? The fact is, the stuff is wonderful. It makes you forget all your problems and—"

"I didn't know being married to me was a big problem," I blurted out, interrupting him. Tears came to my eyes. "I thought we were moving up in the world, that we could be like normal families and leave this life behind!"

Jacques stared at me. "I don't *want* to leave this life behind! I want to live, to feel, to experience life to the fullest!"

"Is that what you're doing when you're all drugged up?" I spat at him. "Experiencing life? That's some reality for you!"

"I didn't know you wanted to make us over to be like your parents!" he rejoined cruelly. "Or maybe your sainted brother!"

"How *dare* you!" I was crying hard now, liquefying the smattering of mascara I had just applied. Jacques turned from me and stalked into our room. I followed him.

"What are you going to do now?" I asked. "What about our baby? I can't possibly pay for the bills alone! Please, Jacques!"

He flung himself on the bed. "Don't worry, Ari. I'll get a new job after I take a little vacation. We've already paid one month's advance rent, so I deserve a rest." He lay back and closed his eyes.

What about me? I wanted to scream at him. *What about* my *rest?* I felt the baby inside of me move restlessly, responding to my emotion, and I forced myself to be calm. "Don't call me Ari," I said through gritted teeth, my voice deceptively calm. "My name is Ariana." Leaving him there on the bed, I turned and ran out the door, pausing only to snatch up my coat from the couch. The October weather was cold, but I was warm from the sparks of our fight. I almost wished I never had to see Jacques again.

I arrived at the cafe slightly late, but Marguerite didn't say anything. She took one look at me and hustled me back to the bathroom, leaving Jules to man the cafe. Working quickly, she cleaned the streaked mascara under my eyes and gave me some powder to cover the red blotches on my face.

"What happened?" she asked softly.

"Jacques and I had our first fight." I nearly started crying again at the words. "He lost his job, and he's taking heroin," I added, searching her face beseechingly. "I don't know what to do. I thought we could make a better life for our baby, but he doesn't seem to want to. At this moment, I wish I'd never met him!"

Marguerite listened intently. "You've good right to be upset. Heroin is addictive and can kill. You must not get involved with it, Ariana, no matter what!" A shadow passed quickly over her face. "You asked me once why I hired you, and I'll tell you now. I had a daughter who hung out with a group like yours. She left home and soon got into heroin and prostitution. She ended up dead." Marguerite paused, and tears rolled down her wrinkled cheeks.

"When you came here, I saw my little girl again, asking for help before she had been drawn into the depths. I couldn't help but think that if someone had been there to help her, she would still be alive today."

The bell hanging on the outside door tinkled suddenly. Then again and again. Marguerite wiped her tears away with the back of her hand.

"I'm so sorry," I whispered, suddenly understanding much more about this woman who had befriended me.

"Just don't let me down," was her reply. She hurried back to the counter to help Jules with the customers, leaving me to follow thoughtfully.

CHAPTER THREE

October went by in a rush of work—for me, anyway. Jacques mostly moped around the apartment in the mornings and complained because I wasn't spending enough time with him. I kept urging him to find a job, but it was a month before he did so. Those first weeks he didn't even try to find a job, but would spend hours with his friends, drinking and shooting up. I knew he was still using heroin, though I didn't know where he got the money. As soon as I got my check, I paid the bills and bought groceries. After that, there was nothing left. Jacques murmured several times that it wasn't right for us to live in such poverty while my parents lived in luxury. He wanted me to ask them for money. "You could say it was for the baby," he suggested several times.

"But I don't want their help!" I exclaimed to him finally. "Besides, they never loved or wanted me; why should they want to give me money?" But even as I said it, happier times when Antoine was alive came to mind. I could see now that they probably had once loved me in their own way. And as for money, the large check they had sent me for my wedding—something I was now grateful I had never told Jacques about—showed they at least felt some responsibility toward me.

"They'd pay just to get you off their backs," he insisted, his sensitivity clouded by his habit.

I sighed. "Jacques, I will not ask my parents for money. You're perfectly healthy, and there's no reason you can't find a job." I wanted to add that even if my parents gave me money, I certainly wouldn't give it to him to spend on drugs. I tried to encourage him, but carefully, so as not to offend his already bruised ego. "You're a good-looking, smart guy," I said, reaching to wrap my arms around his neck and get as close as my huge belly would let me. "There have got to be a hundred companies out there looking for someone like you." I kissed him tenderly and left for work, hours before I should have, bundled up against the increasing November cold.

I walked down the sidewalk, not noticing where I was wandering, and thought about Jacques. He hadn't gotten mad at my suggestion that he find work, like he had all the other times this month. That was a very good sign. Maybe things would work out after all.

I made my way mindlessly to the metro and from there to the Seine, where I sat and watched the boats pass by. From where I was, I could see the Cité—one of the islands that rose in the middle of the Seine. I walked along the parapets and paused at several book stalls but didn't buy anything. Their prices were never low; they sold more to the tourists than the natives. Business was very slow because of the off season, and many of the vendors had simply packed up and left, waiting for spring to return again.

An old woman was selling hot chestnuts from a cart and I eagerly bought some, holding them close to my chest for their warmth. Then I turned back to the Cité, where I could see the tall spires of the Cathédrale da Notre Dame standing out majestically against the more modern lines of the hotel next to it. A feeling of longing overwhelmed me, and I knew that it was for Antoine.

I shrugged off the feeling and began walking, peeling and eating the warm chestnuts as I went. Soon I could see the Palais de Justice. I paused as I always did when seeing it. Somewhere among the buildings lay the Conciergerie, where prisoners like Marie-Antoinette had been held and later beheaded during the French Revolution.

Antoine and I had always loved to hear about the Revolution—how Marie-Antoinette's children had been taken from her and adopted by others, and how Mme. Roland, on the scaffold, had uttered the famous words, "Oh liberty—what crimes are committed in thy name!" We had acted out the parts with passion. But it had all been a game, for neither of us had yet felt the touch of death.

I turned my head quickly from the memories, and raced down the street at a rate quite unbecoming a woman eight months pregnant. I had my head scrunched down in my thick coat that didn't quite reach around my belly—a remnant left over from the easy days with my parents.

I literally ran into them before I even saw them . . . two young men in dark suits and overcoats. For a moment I was scared, until I looked up into their innocent faces filled with concern.

"Uh, excuse me," I said, disengaging myself quickly. I tried futilely to pull my coat lapels together to hide my stomach, and laughed self-consciously when I saw them watching me.

"Well, it's just as well we ran into you," the tallest said in accented French. "I'm Elder Walton, and this is my companion Elder Fredric. We're missionaries from The Church of Jesus Christ of Latter-day Saints, and we have a message to share with you. Do you have a family?"

"Yes," I said suspiciously. I knew without a doubt that they were going to start the foolishness about families being forever like the red-haired boy had done over a year ago, the day of Antoine's funeral. His words had never stopped haunting me, and I didn't want to hear anything else from his friends. I would put a stop to it right now. "But he's dead and gone and you can't bring him back. It's over— now leave me alone!" I skirted around them quickly and continued my wild flight to the metro, resenting them for talking about something that I still so desperately wished could be true.

I made it to the cafe barely on time, throwing myself into my work so as not to think about Jacques, Antoine, or anything serious. But I still felt restless and unhappy. Marguerite looked at me strangely but didn't say anything, letting me work out my own problems. I was grateful for her patience.

Just before the dinner rush, Jacques, with Paulette in tow, came to see me. For once, Jacques' eyes were clear of drugs, unlike Paulette's, whose light-brown eyes were clouded and who moved as if in a dream.

"I got me a job!" Jacques exclaimed, his beautiful smile transforming his features into those of the man I had fallen in love with.

I ran around the counter to hug him. "That's great! What will you be doing?"

"Well, my uncle works for the metro, and he got me a job as a ticket taker. No more heavy lifting for me!" Jacques picked me up and whirled me around somewhat awkwardly.

I felt my happiness flood back. "I'm so happy, Jacques! I knew you could do it!" Jacques swaggered around a bit, basking in my praise like a small child. He kissed me quickly and turned to leave.

"I'm going to tell the gang," he called over his shoulder when he reached the door. His eyes darted to Paulette. "Are you coming?"

She shook her head. "Naw. I came to talk to Ariana. Tell them I'll come by later." Jacques shrugged and left, whistling happily to himself as he walked out into the cold.

I took my break in the kitchen, bringing Paulette with me. "I've only got a few minutes before the rush starts," I said. "Speak fast."

Paulette focused her eyes briefly on me, as if trying to remember what she had come to say. "Oh yeah, it was your parents. I saw them outside your father's bank. They recognized me and asked after you."

"Did you tell them about the baby?" I asked quickly.

She shook her head. "No way. I know you don't want that."

"So what did you tell them? How did they look? Did they ask to see me?" My heart beat rapidly as the questions rushed out one after another, with barely a pause in between.

Paulette closed her eyes for a moment to let the questions sink into her drugged brain. "Let's see. I told them you had a job at a small but very nice cafe, that you and Jacques were still desperately in love, and that you weren't drinking anymore. They asked specifically about that, but I don't think they believed me. And . . . what else did you want to know?"

"How did they look?" I prompted.

"Not good. Older than before—when your brother was—"

"Did they ask to see me?" I interrupted anxiously. "Or say that I was welcome there or something?"

Paulette shook her head. "No."

I sighed. I don't know what I had been expecting. Like me, they were still grieving for Antoine. I, at least, had new hope in my baby.

I glanced out to the counter, where people were beginning to line up. "I've got to go now, but thanks, Paulette." We left the kitchen and I got up on my high stool, watching her leave.

Marguerite was staring at me and I turned my attention to her, raising my eyebrows questioningly.

She pointed to the door with her chin. "That one is just about done for," she said sadly. "She looks like my Michelle the last time I saw her. A few years later, she was dead." Marguerite turned abruptly from me, putting on a mask of happiness for the next customer. But not before I saw the devastating loss in her eyes.

How horrible to lose your only child like that, I thought. My hand went to where my own little one grew, stretching the skin on my stomach so tightly that I feared it would break. *I'll never let you near drugs,* I vowed, setting my jaw firmly. *I'll keep you safe—even if it means keeping you from your own father.*

Wistfully, I turned to my work, masking my thoughts as had Marguerite. Life always went on its speeding course, not caring if one had time to think out the important things.

Jacques kept his job for only a few weeks. He was fired two weeks before Christmas for fighting on the job—not once, but three different times. The company had to pay damages on two of the cases and was taking no more risks with him. His pay for the two weeks had at least taken care of the rent for one more month, as well as the carpet cleaning I insisted on before the baby came, but I had expected much more.

Jacques plunged once more into his drunken, drug-filled world, this time with a vengeance. I withdrew from him, despairing of what I could do to save him and myself.

"What about when the baby comes?" I asked him a couple of days before I was due, a week before Christmas. "I'm not going to be able to work for a few weeks. How will we eat and pay the rent?"

He turned on me. "This whole baby idea wasn't mine," he sneered. "But I did right by marrying you, didn't I? Leave me alone!" He stalked out, slamming the door behind him.

Once more I was late for work, making things worse by bursting into tears the minute I walked in the door. Again Marguerite took me into the back, leaving Jules with the customers. "What did he do this time?" she asked almost menacingly, helping me off with my coat and gloves.

"He got fired, the baby's coming, the doctor tells me that I won't be able to work for two or three weeks . . ." The words came out in a rush as I hiccupped and sobbed my way through my problems.

Marguerite listened sympathetically. When I had calmed somewhat she said, "Well, your doctor is right. I remember with my Michelle, I was in bed for a week and couldn't walk without pain for another two. They told me that second babies are better though, so remember that it shouldn't be so bad the next time."

"The *next* time?" The idea sounded so ridiculous that I laughed in spite of myself. I had learned a thing or two in the last nine months, and there was no way I was going to have another baby until Jacques straightened out completely.

Marguerite smiled. "And Ariana, you don't have to worry about how to pay your rent. You have become very valuable to us. Your quickness and friendly ways have increased business substantially, and we've decided to raise your wage. You can also take your vacation with pay earlier, instead of after a year's work, so you can receive money while on maternity leave. And when you get well, you can bring the baby with you to work. We'll put a crib in the office where the cot is, and you can come and nurse or take care of him or her anytime you want. Jules and I will help you."

I threw my arms around Marguerite. "Oh, thank you! How can I ever repay you?"

Marguerite sniffed. "You have already become the daughter I lost, and I am very proud of you. I should have told you before this, but . . ." She shrugged as her voice trailed off. We sat in comfortable silence, and then she spoke again.

"There's one more thing, Ariana. We have several small, one bedroom apartments above us that are or will soon be vacant. I know you want a better environment for your child, and while our building is old, it is well cared for and the renters very carefully screened. We would offer you a rent as low as your other place if you want to move here, but . . ."—she hesitated as if choosing her words carefully— ". . . we wouldn't accept anyone on drugs."

I nodded, knowing that she meant Jacques. "Thank you, Marguerite. I am very grateful to you and I will think about it, but I do mean to stay with my husband, if I can. I still love him."

Marguerite stood up. "I understand that, Ariana," she said softly. "I simply wanted you to be aware of an alternative if you should come to need it."

We went to work, relieving Jules, who was swamped with orders. Together Marguerite and I handled the rush easily, talking naturally with our customers, most of whom we knew by name. Through the afternoon, I felt my stomach tighten and relax as it had been doing for the last week. False labor, they called it, and while it wasn't really painful, it did give me a sense of what was to come.

In the late afternoon, I noticed the contractions were coming at regular fifteen-minute intervals. They still seemed no harder or more painful than before, but it drove me to distraction. Could the baby be coming?

The dinner rush was hectic as usual, and I worked as quickly as possible to take the customers' orders. During any slowdown, no matter how brief, Marguerite or I would slip over to the dining area to clear the tables. At first, I didn't notice that the contractions were coming even closer and more severely, causing me to catch my breath. I thought I was just tired from the long day. Then, all at once, I doubled up in pain near a table I was wiping clean. I sat abruptly on the chair, surprise covering my face. I knew without a doubt that I was in real labor. There could be no mistaking it; I understood at that moment that false labor was as much like real labor as a simple wren resembled the majestic bald eagle.

"Marguerite!" I shouted, oblivious to the many curious stares turned my way. My pain and excitement must have been written on my face, because she dropped what she was doing immediately.

"We're closing early tonight!" she pronounced loudly. "Ariana's going to have her baby!" Everyone clapped, and a few regulars crowded around me. Marguerite brought my coat and helped me into it.

"You take her to the hospital," Jules said. "I'll close and see if I can find Jacques before I follow you." He put his hand on the shoulder of one of the regulars. "Will you take them in your car?" The man nodded, and he and Marguerite helped me out the door into the freezing night air.

As we left, I noticed that someone had already put up the "Closed" sign on the door to the cafe, with a bigger one beneath that read: "Ariana's having her baby!"

I remember little of the mad dash through Paris to the hospital, only the pain that seemed to come and go like waves in the ocean. I do remember calling Antoine's name and my mother's, but neither was there to help me. Just Marguerite, whose rough hand clasped mine and helped me through the pain.

When we got to the hospital, I was already fully dilated. The doctor told me I had probably been in labor since the early afternoon yet hadn't recognized it. He offered me some drugs to dull the pain, though he was doubtful they would take effect before the baby came. Regardless, I refused. There was no way I would allow any drugs into my body—especially when I knew they would go into my baby as well, dulling his or her first precious moments of life. Besides, I figured Jacques already used more than enough drugs for his whole family.

I didn't once think of my husband as I pushed and pushed, feeling that my insides were about to explode. Through it all, Marguerite was a solid rock in my storm. Sometime near the end, Jacques came into the room. His eyes were glazed and he reeked of alcohol. For an instant I was happy to see him, until I realized that he was mostly unaware of what was happening. When he suddenly leaned over and retched on the floor, I had had enough.

I glared at him angrily. "Not even for this could you be sober! Get out! I don't want you here to sully our baby with your drugged company!" Anger flared briefly in his eyes, but he turned and left without uttering a single word.

Someone cleaned up the mess while I tried to rest in between contractions, which were coming more quickly by the moment. Soon I could no longer tell when one ended and the other began.

"I can see the head now, Ariana," the doctor said suddenly. "Just a couple more big pushes, and it'll be out."

My labor had already gone on much longer than the doctor had expected, and I was exhausted. Still, I gathered up my scattered energy and pushed for all I was worth. It was closer to five pushes before the head was free, followed immediately by the body. I felt relief flood through me—never had I known such a wonderful feeling!

"You have a little girl," the doctor said, bringing the baby to me. "Healthy and beautiful."

I knew as he spoke that I had wanted a girl all along. I hadn't been able to afford an ultrasound to determine the sex of my child, but in my dreams, the baby had always been a girl. "Oh, my precious Antoinette," I cooed. "You're so beautiful! I've waited so long for you!"

"She's so perfect!" Marguerite exclaimed.

We sat there looking down in speechless awe at my baby for long minutes, until the doctor whisked her away for a few tests. I felt a great loss when they took her from me, almost an ache. But before I knew it, she was back again in my arms, and Marguerite was showing me how to nurse her.

A sudden commotion came from down the hall as Jacques pushed past Jules, who was guarding the waiting room door. "It's my baby too!" he yelled. "And I want to see her!"

I was afraid of what I would see when he barged his way in, but someone had given him lots of coffee and made him shower and change. There was only a trace of the drugs in his eyes, and not even the smell remained of the alcohol.

Jacques stared at the baby in amazement. "She's so tiny, so beautiful," he whispered reverently. He reached out to glide a finger over the baby's cheek.

"Would you like to hold her?" I asked, keeping the reluctance from my voice.

Jacques stared at the baby for a minute before replying. "May I?" I nodded and carefully handed Antoinette to him. As I did so, she opened her dark eyes to gaze into his. Wonder spread over his face. I felt happiness in my heart as I watched my husband tenderly cuddle our daughter, our little angel from heaven. Sighing, I lay back on the pillows. From the corner of my eye, I caught a glimpse of Jules hovering outside my room.

"Jules, come in here and see the baby," I called. He came eagerly with the same reverence on his face that Jacques had shown.

After a few minutes, Jacques awkwardly handed the baby back to me. "I think she's hungry, she's trying to suck on her fist," he said. I gratefully took my daughter back into my arms.

"I didn't know what it would be like," Jacques continued, his voice clearly showing his amazement. "I had no idea I would feel this way." He tore his gaze from Antoinette and looked at me earnestly. "I do want to be worthy of her—and you, Ariana. I'll make good, you'll see. I'm through with drugs."

I knew he was sincere, and I wanted to believe him. But something told me that such a change wouldn't come easily.

Chapter Four

"I got a job!" Jacques exclaimed triumphantly the day before Christmas. Little Nette was six days old. I felt a sense of déjà-vu; this was the third time Jacques had said this exact phrase to me since I first met him, once before our marriage and twice since. I wondered how long this job would last.

I stifled the thought quickly. "That's great, honey!" I said. "Doing what?"

"I'm a doorman at that hotel near Notre Dame!"

I was surprised. "Why, that's really something! I can't believe it! How did you do it?"

He told me in detail, but my thoughts wandered as he spoke. It didn't matter how he had charmed his way into the job, just that he had gotten it. The week since Nette's birth had passed in a sea of happiness for me, marred only by the fear that Jacques would not live up to his promise. But each day he had searched diligently for work, and then had come home to attend to Nette and me faithfully. I hadn't seen him drugged up or drinking the whole week, though I had smelled alcohol on his breath a time or two, and was happy that he seemed to be keeping his promise. I was proud of Jacques, and felt all the love I had for my handsome husband brimming to the surface again.

While I was happy with Jacques and basked in his tender care, I still felt afraid to trust and love him completely. With my precious new baby, I had no such reserves. I delighted in Nette, and lavished

upon her all the love I felt I hadn't received from my own mother—
all the love I had once cherished only for my twin brother. She was a
miracle, and I couldn't believe the incredible love and awe that
glowed in my heart each time I looked at her soft, perfect features. I
gave her my whole love as only a mother can. In return, she was a
good baby, fussing only when she was hungry or cold.

I was relieved to have my own body back after being pregnant for
so long, though my breasts were sore and cracked from nursing. I
shrugged the pain aside, knowing it would not last.

"How about a party to celebrate my new job?" Jacques suggested,
coming to sit with me on our old couch. He had finished a very
prolonged explanation of how he convinced the manager at the hotel
to hire him, a feat that included showing pictures of me and little
Antoinette.

While I hadn't been listening closely to his story, I stiffened
immediately at the mention of a party. "I don't think that's a good
idea, Jacques," I protested, choosing my words carefully. "The baby is
too young to be exposed to all that smoke and excitement."

Jacques looked doubtful, but still seemed determined to do what
was best for his daughter. "Well, maybe you're right. We can have a
party in a few weeks, when she's older."

So we spent a quiet and happy Christmas, cuddling together
against the cold outside that seeped in through the thin windows and
walls. We bought each other very small gifts—a new pair of gloves
for me and a wallet for Jacques—and we ate Christmas dinner with
Marguerite and Jules. Because of the baby, we all agreed to have
dinner on Christmas Day instead of the traditional one at midnight
on Christmas Eve. For presents, Marguerite and Jules gave us clothes
for Antoinette, and I happily dressed her up in each outfit to model
for us while Jules snapped photographs. To my wonder, Jacques was
charming and full of fun; even Marguerite was impressed with him.

The next week sped by quickly. Paulette and Marguerite came to
see me often, cooing and cuddling the baby. I loved Marguerite's
visits, but I was always nervous to let Paulette hold Nette. She was
more often drugged than not, and I was afraid she would drop the
baby. I didn't let the rest of our gang in the apartment at all, using
the sleeping baby and my recovery as an excuse; but the better I got,

the harder it was to keep them out. It helped that Jacques worked mostly nights; I found that I simply could not answer the door when they came, justifying my actions because of Antoinette.

When little Nette was two weeks old I returned to work. I felt good, though I still tired easily. "That's because you're nursing," Marguerite said as she showed me the small crib with wheels that she and Jules had purchased. "See? It rolls. That way if she's awake, we can roll her into the kitchen to be with Jules while he's cooking, or even to the counter with us if we're not too busy. Of course, when she's a little older we'll have to block off part of the kitchen and put some blankets down to let her crawl—we can't have her growing up confined to a crib, you know."

Her expression was serious and I laughed. "Yes, I know, Marguerite, and I'll be careful never to leave her in a crib too much at home." I didn't tell Marguerite that I didn't even have a crib for Nette at the apartment, that she slept peacefully next to me on our bed. This made it easier for night nursings, and Jacques and I both loved to cuddle with her.

At first it was difficult for me to leave Nette in the office or kitchen. It was as if a part of me was missing—and I guess in a way it was; Nette, after all, had been a part of me for nine months. She slept most of the time, and the few times she was fussy I carried her next to my chest in a baby carrier, or Jules sang to her in the kitchen. I was very happy.

We had more customers than ever that week, as many people were still on holiday from work or school. News about the baby spread quickly, and nearly everyone insisted on seeing her. Many of the regulars brought gifts. "Where is that baby?" people would say as they approached the counter. Then I would proudly show her off. "She looks just like you with that dark hair and big brown eyes," they would always continue. I thought that she did too, though she had her father's slight cleft in her tiny chin.

My life seemed perfect. Oh, I still complained about my apartment and secretly missed my parents, but I was so full of wonder and love for my daughter that those things made little difference. To me, it seemed almost as if my beloved brother had been restored to me in the form of a baby, though I did not believe that exactly.

Jacques had been at his job for three weeks when he brought up the party again. We were spending a quiet night alone in front of the TV. For once it hadn't been busy at the cafe, and Marguerite had sent me home early. Little Nette was already asleep on our bed.

"Let's have a party to show off the baby," he said abruptly.

"But the smoke—"

"We won't let anyone smoke—pot or tobacco. Afterwards, they can move down to one of the bars. Or," he cast me a boyish glance, "they can do it in the hall."

"Okay," I agreed reluctantly, seeing his excitement and determination in the matter. "But no drugs, no shooting up. Not around the baby."

"It's a deal! Tomorrow night, then. It's Sunday and we're both off." He jumped up abruptly, glancing at his watch.

"Where are you going?"

"To get some drinks for the party. The liquor store is still open. And I'll call a few of the guys to spread the word." He threw on his coat and shot out the door.

I was left alone.

"This is one hoppin' party!" a man shouted at me above the dance music. I tried not to wince at the reeking smell of alcohol on his breath.

I nodded and turned abruptly to search the crowd for Jacques. The front room and kitchen were full of people, half of whom I had never even met. They were dancing, necking, playing cards, and drinking. So far, they had all scrupulously obeyed Jacques when he said no smoking or drugs in the house, but it had made little difference. They went just outside in the hall to do both, leaving the door wide open so the smoke drifted into the apartment. Many of our guests were already passed out in the hall and on our floor.

"Have you seen Jacques?" I asked Paulette when I found her sitting in the hall, squeezed in among many others.

"In the kitchen, last I saw," Paulette said. "But relax, Ariana. He's just having a good time celebrating his new job and Nette. Loosen up a little and have some fun, like in the good old days before you got pregnant." She pointed down at a needle in her hand. "Want a little?"

"No!" I said tightly. I had already taken a few drinks, but quit when I started to feel dizzy. I couldn't risk not being able to take care of Nette should she need me.

I found Jacques in a crowded corner of the kitchen as Paulette had said, having a drinking contest with five of his friends. I saw at once that he was already too far gone to move the party to a bar somewhere, but still I tried.

"Jacques, it's time to go to the bar!" I shouted above the din.

He stared at me dumbly for a few moments, as if trying to remember who I was. "Oh, it's you, Ariana," he said finally. "Have a drink?" He held up his glass with an unsteady hand.

I turned away, disgusted, making my way as quickly as possible to our small bedroom where I had left Nette after her brief, one-minute introduction to her father's friends. I had made sure the room was off limits, marking it with a large sign and verbal threats. So far no one had dared enter, but I was afraid to leave Nette for very long; these were people who thrived on breaking the rules. Fleetingly, I wondered what I had ever seen in such a life.

But as I pushed through the thick mass of bodies, a sinking despair flooded through me. *Is this what life is all about?* I thought. I was suddenly tempted to throw myself into the party, to drink myself crazy so that I could get rid of this growing hopelessness. But the thought of my precious Nette saved me.

I finally reached the bedroom and opened the door. My anger flared as I saw a couple wrestling around on my bed, threatening at any second to roll over my one-month-old daughter. I raced up to the bed, fury and fear flooding my mind and body, blotting out the former despair; it was a savage blaze, ripping through my soul. Abruptly, I was the fear-strengthened mother protecting her young.

"Get out!" I screamed, pulling them off the bed and onto the floor with a strength I didn't know I possessed. They landed with a bump and a chorus of complaints. "Get out of my room!" I yelled again. I wanted to scream stronger words at them, words that until then I hadn't realized I even knew; but ever conscious of my little daughter, I refrained. Grabbing the couple by the collars of their t-shirts, I hauled them over to the door, practically strangling them. They were too weak with drugs and drinking to protest much. I reached to open the door to shove them out. As I did so, two more couples burst in.

"Not in here!" I shrieked. "I swear I'll call the police!" That finally got them all out the door, but I knew it wouldn't keep them for long.

At once, I swept over to the bed to make sure Nette was all right. I was still so furious that I was shaking, but I forced myself to focus on what to do next. We had to get out of the apartment. I dressed the baby as quickly as possible in her warm body coat, shoving extra items into the baby bag someone had given me. Nette's eyes opened and her lips curled in a sweet, angelic smile.

"I'm getting you out of here, Nette," I whispered. She closed her eyes trustingly, already dozing off again to dream of things that babies dream, special visions veiled from the knowledge of adults.

I added an extra layer to my own clothing and wrapped Nette in two more blankets to protect her from the winter cold. We left quickly, stopping only at the closet to get my own coat. From the corner of my eye, I saw another couple head toward my room. Anger again flared in me, but getting Nette somewhere safe was more important now. I shrugged and turned my back resolutely on the crowded apartment. No one paid any attention to us as we left.

Though it rarely snowed in Paris, it did get very cold in the winter months. This January night was no exception. An icy wind was blowing furiously outside and I put Nette inside my coat, making sure she could still breathe but protecting her face from the biting wind. "We'll go to Marguerite's," I said softly to the baby, though she was asleep. "Only two blocks away." I watched the shadows carefully as I hurried down the sidewalk. These streets were not the safest at this hour, and I had never walked them alone after dark. Either Jules or Jacques had always walked me home after my shift at the cafe. Cold fear arose in me, but I didn't know what else to do.

All at once, I remembered the red-haired American missionary and thought, *Now's the time I really need a prayer.* But I didn't pray for myself, at least not consciously. Nette's coming had made me rethink my former disbelief in God, but I hadn't yet figured out exactly what I did believe.

As I neared the cafe, I realized that someone was following us. "Please, let us make it," I mumbled, not realizing that such a fervent wish was actually a prayer. We arrived at the cafe, and I began to ring the buzzer insistently. I could now see three youths coming down the street, angling for where I stood. My heart beat wildly as I thought about what I should do. *Should I run? Face them? What?* I pushed again and again on the buzzer, then turned to face my attackers. I felt helpless to protect myself and my daughter.

"What's a pretty thing like you doing all alone on a night like this?" one asked as they neared. "We can help you out!"

"I don't need help, thank you," I said stiffly, trying to hide my fear. Inside my coat, Nette began to wriggle in her sleep, and I shifted her position awkwardly.

"Hey now, what you got inside that coat?" the youth asked, genuinely curious, but menacing as well. I knew in a moment he would rip my coat open to see for himself.

At that moment, the door opened behind me and Jules appeared. He sized up the situation immediately and turned a gruff face to the boys, holding up a large fist. "Go on now, I'll take care of my daughter. Or do you want my wife," he motioned to Marguerite, who had appeared at the counter behind him, "to call the police while we fight about it?"

The boys examined Jules, who was short but strong-looking, and backed down. "We don't want any trouble, mister," said the one who had spoken before. "We just wanted to make sure she got in okay."

"Yeah, right," Jules said, his voice full of irony. He whisked me inside and closed the door in their faces.

"What's wrong?" Marguerite came to me quickly as Jules locked up.

I began to shake with delayed fright. "Here, take Nette," I said, holding out the baby. I was suddenly afraid I would drop her. As Marguerite swept the sleeping baby up to her warm breast, I began to tell my story. "Can I stay here tonight?" I said when I had finished.

"Of course." Marguerite led the way through the kitchen to their own apartment. I had been there only a few times before, but I knew they had a couch that folded down into a bed in their sitting room. It was to this that she took me.

"What's wrong with my life?" I asked her while she made up the bed. I was sitting back in a comfortable chair with Nette asleep on my chest. "I don't know what to do!"

Marguerite stopped what she was doing and looked down at me. "It seems you have a lot of decisions to make, Ariana. You still have your whole life before you."

"What would you do if you were me?" I asked softly.

She shook her head. "Only you can decide that. But you might start with deciding where you want to end up in life, and work from there. To get there, you might have to go back to school, make up with your parents, maybe make some decisions about Jacques. But the point is, only you can do it."

I frowned, then nodded. "I guess you're right."

Suddenly out of nowhere came the thought, *Oh, Antoine, why did you leave me?*

CHAPTER FIVE

The next day the biting wind continued, but it didn't seem to stop the flow of people to the cafe. I was grateful that I could immerse myself in work, putting aside my feelings and the decisions I would soon have to make. Regardless, I felt their weight heavy upon me as sin upon the soul.

Jacques didn't appear all morning or afternoon, but shortly before the dinner rush, Paulette came in, her face flushed and excited.

"Boy, did you miss all of the excitement last night!" she declared, leaning against the counter. "Someone called the police, and the whole place got busted. They took most everyone to the tank, including Jacques. I didn't get busted because I slipped into one of your neighbors' apartments. You know, the ones that have that so-called band. Anyway, I went down to the jail to see what was what and Jacques was there, asking you to come and bail him out."

I stared at Paulette in horror, then looked to Marguerite for advice.

She shrugged. "Honey, if it was up to me, I'd let him rot in jail. But it's you that has to live with him, not me. However, if you're going to get him out, it would be best if you went now, before the dinner rush. That way maybe he won't lose his job."

"Yes, you're right. Will you watch the baby for me?"

"Sure." Marguerite's eyes fixed on me sadly. "Do you have enough money?"

"I think so." I wasn't sure if I did, but I wasn't about to ask her for more than she was already giving me. If I had to, I would take some money out of my secret bank account.

Paulette and I hurried up the street to the metro. The sky was overcast and gloomy. A perfect day for what I had to do. I had enough cash to pay the police officer to get Jacques free. It was money I had been saving to pay the rent that was due in just over a week.

"What about the rent, Jacques?" I asked tightly.

"When's it due?"

"End of next week." I couldn't believe that he didn't remember.

"Then it's no problem," Jacques said confidently. "I get paid next week. We'll have enough to pay the rent. Don't worry about that, Ari."

"Ariana," I corrected him tersely.

"Oh, sorry." He turned to Paulette. "But wasn't that some party, eh, Paulette?"

"Sure was," she agreed, a stupid smile on her face.

I stopped dead in my tracks. "I don't believe you, Jacques! There was smoke filling the whole apartment, drunken and doped people everywhere, couples making out on our bed, practically rolling on top of Nette! Then Nette and I nearly get mugged or worse in the street trying to find someplace to sleep, and you end up in jail! And you call that a party?" I let all of my pent-up anger out in one rush, and Jacques cringed in the face of my rage. "Is that how you want your daughter to grow up? Doing drugs and sleeping with whoever is available? Well, that's not the kind of life *I* want for her—or for me! I want to grow up and get on with living, and if that's not what you want, then you can have your drugged life. But it's us or them, you can't have both!" With that I turned on my heel, leaving a stunned Jacques behind me.

I spent the rest of the day angry at Jacques, but gradually my rage cooled. At closing time, he appeared with flowers to walk me home. Jules and Marguerite scowled at him suspiciously, but he seemed clear-headed.

"I thought a lot about what you said," he began when we were in the street. "You know, about what kind of a life we want for Antoinette." He motioned to the baby in my arms. "You're right, I don't want her to grow up like this, and I don't even want this life for you and me." His eyes grew thoughtful. "Like at Christmas, when we ate dinner with Marguerite and Jules, I thought how it would be having a place like that, and doing well like they are. I really want that for us, but sometimes the yearning to drink comes so hard that I just can't fight it. And the heroin is worse," he held up his hands quickly, "though I swear I haven't done it but once or twice since Nette was born.

"But the whole point is that I'm going to do better, Ariana. I promise." He put a hesitant arm around me and I leaned into him slightly.

"Okay, Jacques, we'll try it again. But no more parties."

"I agree. And we'll look for someplace nicer to live, now that we both have jobs."

"Maybe we should go back to school," I suggested.

"Maybe."

But I could tell that he was humoring me. He was sincere in wanting to do better, but that didn't include being locked up in a room with books. I sighed. I guess it was all I could expect, for now.

I seemed to hold my breath as the next two months passed by. Jacques was impossibly well behaved. We laughed a lot and spent a lot of time as a family. During March, as the weather warmed, I would even take him to some of my favorite places along the Seine, recounting the stories of my youth.

"You were very lucky to have Antoine," Jacques said to me one day as we walked along the river. It was the morning before my nineteenth birthday. "I feel almost jealous when you talk about him. Your whole face lights up, and you look more beautiful than ever. I hope I can make your eyes light up like that someday."

My hair, having grown long during my pregnancy, fell into my face, and I flipped it back to look up at him. "I do love you, Jacques," I said earnestly. "I really do! These last two months have been good for us, haven't they?"

His expression was serious. "The best in my whole life." But as he said it, a shadow passed over his face. "I wish that—" He broke off suddenly. "Oh, look at the time! We've got to get to work!" He kissed me tenderly and took Nette from my arms and kissed her, too. Together we headed toward the metro.

I hummed as I worked that afternoon, noticing how the sun shone through the window, casting a glow about the cafe. I was happy, but something whispered menacingly that it was too good to last. I pushed the thought away forcefully; problems came easily enough without my searching for them.

But the feeling had been right; things were too good to be true. Paulette came into the cafe after lunch and dropped the bomb. Her words exploded in my heart and broke the tentative trust I had developed in Jacques.

"I have something I think I should tell you," she said, staring at me unhappily from across the small table in the kitchen where we sat. I froze instantly. Nette, in my arms, felt the difference and looked up at my face curiously.

"What is it, Paulette? Is it Jacques?" I asked quickly, trying hard to breathe normally. I remembered only too vividly the problems Jacques and I had gone through before Nette's birth.

She nodded. "I'm really sorry, Ariana, and I shouldn't be the one to tell you, but you deserve to know." She avoided my gaze as she rushed on quickly. "Jacques quit his job about three weeks ago. He said he was tired of being treated like a servant."

I shut my eyes and breathed deeply. Still, if that was all, maybe we could . . .

"And that's not all," Paulette continued as if reading my thoughts. "He's been with the gang during the day, drugged up like the rest of us. He does it early in the day, and it wears off a bit so he can still walk you home without you noticing too much. Then he sleeps it off." Her voice grew quiet. "He sometimes brags about fooling you, and I just couldn't stand it any longer. Even though you aren't really one of us anymore, you'll always be my friend."

I thought about what she was saying carefully. Jacques had been quiet at night, and I had felt he was hiding something from me—but drugs? *How could I be that blind?*

"I guess I wanted to believe him," I said despondently, more to myself than to Paulette.

"Today I asked him what he was going to do for money." Paulette obviously wasn't finished with her story, and I steeled myself for more. "He said that he'd just live off his old woman—don't take offense, it was the drugs talking. Then he said that maybe he'd find an easier way to live." Paulette met my gaze straight on. "Ariana, I think he went to see your parents."

Anger erupted inside me. *How dare he beg for money when he wasn't willing to work for it!*

The rest of the day, I practiced in my mind the things I would say to him when he came to pick me up. But after closing he didn't come, and Jules ended up walking me home. It began to rain, and I was reminded again of Antoine.

Jacques was not in the apartment when I arrived. After putting Nette to bed, I paced the floor restlessly, waiting in the dim lamplight for my husband's return. I knew our marriage was ended, that we had to separate, at least until he got his head on straight, but I didn't know if I would have the courage to tell him. Somehow, for my daughter, I had to be strong.

Sometime after one o'clock in the morning, Jacques stumbled in. He didn't see me at first, but when he did, he held open his arms.

"Hi, honey."

I didn't move to greet him. "You lied to me."

Jacques stopped short. "I didn't want you to worry about the job. I'll find a better one."

"Will you? And what about the drugs, Jacques? You said that you were finished with the drugs!"

"I am," he said innocently.

"Oh? Then you won't mind if I take a look for myself." I turned the brighter overhead lights on while Jacques covered his eyes at the sudden glare. I pushed his hands away from his face, and saw what I had tried so hard not to see these past months. I checked his coat pockets and found the hard evidence.

"No wonder we don't have any money!" I shouted, holding the drugs in front of his face. "You spend it all on drugs, even when you're working! Well, I can't do it anymore! I can't support you and your habit! You see only what you want to see—you're blinded by the drugs! Don't you know that I need you, that I love you?" I shook my head. "But not like this."

"We've got plenty of money, Ariana," Jacques responded coldly. He pulled his wallet out of his pocket to reveal a fat sheaf of large bills.

My eyes opened wide. "Where did you get this?"

"Little Ariana, pretending to be so innocent," he said mockingly. "I got this money where you got yours, though I don't know where you've kept it all this time. I got it from your parents. I told them about our baby and how we desperately needed the money. Your father wanted to know what we did with all the other money he gave us for our wedding. Remember that, dear Ariana? I told him we had to pay extra hospital bills when the baby was born, because of complications. But now you tell me, what did you do with the money?"

"I was saving it for the baby! Or for an emergency!" I exclaimed. "What would you have done with it? Tell me, Jacques! No, let me tell you. You would have had a party, or spent it on drugs. You certainly wouldn't have wanted to work at all," I said bitterly. "Just like you're doing now. I wanted us to make something better of ourselves, not only for our baby, but for us! I wanted you and me to spend that money to help us in school, but you just want to waste your life away!"

His face became livid. "No, Ariana," he hissed through clenched teeth, "that's what I *have* been doing—wasting my time away here with you, when I could be out really living and enjoying myself!"

That stung, because despite our problems, I believed Jacques was staying with me because he loved me. "Okay, maybe I was wrong not to tell you about the money," I admitted reluctantly, trying to see his point. "But I wasn't wrong in what I wanted to do with it."

"It doesn't matter anymore, Ariana," Jacques said firmly. "I'm leaving."

My laugh was short and bitter. "That's funny, I was going to tell you the same thing." But it didn't feel funny. It hurt almost as bad as Antoine's death.

He looked at me. "We'll, I guess there's nothing more to say."

"I guess not." Then I added more softly, "But tell me one thing. This morning you said these past few months were the best you'd ever spent. Was that also a lie?"

I could tell he wanted to say that it was, but he couldn't. "It's true, Ariana. I got a glimpse of the life we could have had together under other circumstances. But I'm not good enough for you, and I don't know if I want to be."

"And Nette?"

He shook his head. "She's better off without me." At that he scooped up his wallet and all the bills. Draping his coat over his arm, he headed for the door. "Tell your parents thanks for the money," he said over his shoulder. "They know our address and will probably show up here one day. They wanted to see the baby."

Then he was gone and I was left alone again, listening to the rain falling in the empty streets.

CHAPTER SIX

The morning of my nineteenth birthday dawned, though I had surely thought that after my separation from Jacques nothing in the world could possibly be the same. I awoke early, and without thinking felt the side of the bed where he slept. Of course it was empty. I looked down at Nette sleeping peacefully beside me, her little body curled into mine. A deep sadness filled my heart. As my father had distanced himself from me a year and a half ago at Antoine's death, so had my baby's father distanced himself from her, and just as permanently.

Listlessness settled upon me, and I didn't want to even get out of bed. I lay there for an hour, gazing alternately at the ceiling and my sleeping baby. Then she stretched and slowly open her eyes, looking up at me with such love and trust that it forced me to think seriously about our future.

"We're all alone, Nette," I said to her softly. "But that's okay because we have each other, and women have been raising children without men since time began." I bit my lip, unwilling to let my child see how much the thought frightened me, though I knew she wouldn't understand. Nette smiled and giggled softly, reaching up to put her hand in my mouth.

Suddenly a loud shout came through the thin walls. Some of my neighbors were fighting, even this early in the morning. Abruptly, I made my decision.

"The first thing to do is get out of this hole," I said, bringing

Nette to my breast to nurse. "After you eat, we'll get up and bathe and see if Marguerite still has an apartment for us." Strength and determination cascaded through my body. Tears were for late, rainy nights, but days were for action.

Less than an hour later, we were at the cafe. It was also open for breakfast, but they had another girl, Dauphine, helping out in the mornings, so Marguerite was free to talk with me when I arrived.

"What? Here so early?" she asked with a smile, reaching out to hug and kiss Nette. "How about some breakfast—on the house?"

I returned her smile. "No thanks, I've already eaten. But what Nette and I do need is a small apartment, if you've got one open. Jacques and I have separated."

Marguerite watched me without speaking for a moment, then said quietly, "I'm sorry, Ariana. It's a rotten thing to have happen on your birthday, but maybe you can see it as a new birth or something."

I bit my lip hard so my new strength wouldn't suddenly fail me. "That's how I'm looking at it. I'm starting anew. I'm going to go back to school, too, if I can find a program that will allow me to do much of the studying at home with Nette, and then on to college. We're going to build our own life, Nette and I."

Marguerite hugged us both. "Good for you! I'll be here to help you out. And I will have an apartment free next week. I've been inter- viewing people for it, but haven't promised it to anyone yet. So it's yours, and half-price this month because of your birthday!"

"Oh, thank you, Marguerite!"

I had a few hours before work, so I searched out a couple of schools in the area. Because of my age and the baby, it was relatively easy to find a program that would work around my schedule. The program I chose would begin in a month, and I could learn at home and take the tests when I was finished. I had to use a good chunk of my parents' wedding gift to pay for it, but I knew it would be worth it in the long run. I figured it would only take me four months to finish my last year of high school, even with only mornings to study. Of course, I would have to find someone to watch Nette during the tests, but I was sure Marguerite and Jules would help.

I had time afterwards to walk by some of my favorite spots along the Seine. When we arrived near the Palais de Justice, I told little Nette the story of Queen Marie-Antoinette. "She must have been very beautiful, as you are going to be," I concluded. "But the point is that she was a queen, and that's what we are both going to be. That's one of the reasons I named you Antoinette, you know. I want you to be as wonderful as my brother, Antoine, and as noble as a queen. Not the kind who rules over others, but the kind who rules herself and is not afraid to love and be kind, even though it sometimes hurts so much." Sorrow and pain clutched at my heart when I thought about how much I was hurting for those I had lost. But I blinked back the tears quickly and walked on.

I stopped at one of the vendors along the river and bought a stuffed bear for Nette. It was fluffy and as white as snow, and so cuddly. She grabbed at it immediately, smiling, but shortly lost interest. I didn't mind; I knew that as she grew older she would learn to love it as much as I had once loved my own stuffed bear, now long gone.

I kept walking until I found a bench where I could sit down. Though Nette was only three months old, I had been lugging her around all morning and was beginning to feel even her slight weight. She had fallen abruptly asleep as she always seemed to do, but I was content to look down on her peaceful, angelic face. Emotion welled up in my heart, and I knew I loved her more than I had ever loved anyone in my entire life, including Antoine. She was a perfect miracle.

After a while I heard singing from a distance, and my curiosity made me go see what it was. Several young men and woman like those I had seen the day of Antoine's funeral were singing. They held up a sign as before about families being eternal, and also another one that read: "Jesus Christ Loves You!"

Strangely, I felt a warm glow inside of me. I once had decided that God didn't live because Antoine had died; but now I had little Nette, and the love I felt for her was so strong that I couldn't help wondering if God had sent her to me. Maybe he existed after all.

"Oh, Nette," I whispered to the sleeping baby. "I wish it were all true, that we could see Antoine again somehow, and that you could be mine forever."

Glancing at my watch, I suddenly realized I was late for work and hurried in the direction of the metro. A young woman held a pamphlet out to me as I passed, and I hurriedly took it and shoved it into my coat pocket. It was well and good to dream, but I had to come back to the real world now. There was work to be done.

A week later, Jules and Marguerite helped me move my few belongings to the new apartment. They absolutely refused to let me keep the couch, however, saying that it was flea-infested and dirty beyond saving. "We have one that you can have," Marguerite said. "I ordered a new one for our apartment only last week to go with the new wallpaper, and the old one has to go."

"You mean the beautiful one with the bed in it?" I asked. She nodded. "Well, in that case, let's leave the old bed behind, too," I said. "We'll sleep on the couch-bed until we can buy one of our own. I—I think it would be easier for me if I didn't have the same bed."

"Well, I can certainly understand that," Marguerite agreed immediately. "And that's one less thing we'll have to move!"

We did take the small kitchen table with its two chairs, the TV, the TV stand, the lamp and corner table, and the crates I had been using to store our clothes. It wasn't much, but it was enough.

The new apartment was everything I could have wished for. It was as small as the one we'd come from, except for the bathroom, which was twice the size. It had new-looking carpet and vinyl flooring, and the walls had been freshly painted. Everything had a clean look and smell about it which made me love it immediately. I wasn't afraid to let Nette on the floor, even though she always rolled off her blanket.

During the moving, Marguerite and Jules kept disappearing and reappearing with odds and ends to make the apartment more comfortable. "This dresser was left in one of the apartments last year," Jules said once. "It needs a little paint, but it'll be better than those crates for your clothes."

About the same time, Marguerite came in with some wall hangings. "I bought these just last month, but they didn't go with the new wallpaper."

On and on they went until my apartment really did look like a home. Not even once did I let myself think about Jacques; that part of my life was over. Only at night was I unable to forget, and then I cried. But morning would soon dawn, and I would start anew.

A week later, my parents showed up at the cafe. It was during the evening rush, so I pretended I hadn't seen them and worked furiously, hoping they would go away. But they waited until things slowed down.

"Who are they?" Marguerite asked, smoothing her white apron over her large bosom.

I grimaced. "My parents."

"Well, they don't seem too bad," Marguerite said.

I looked at them, trying to see them from her point of view, but all I could see were the cold faces that had shut me out of their lives when my beloved brother had died.

"I don't want to see them," I whispered suddenly.

But Marguerite wouldn't let me run away. "You're going to have to face them sometime. Remember that they not only lost Antoine, but you as well. They've got to be hurting. Try to be nice to them." Her words reminded me of how I had told Nette on my birthday that we were going to be queens. I guess it was now time for me to act like one.

I wiped my hands and went over to the door where they waited. "Hello," I said, trying to make my voice as steady as possible.

"Hello, Ariana," my mother said quickly. "You look good. I like your hair long like that."

"We went to your old apartment and they told us that you work here, so we came," my father added. "We wanted to see how you were doing."

"I'm fine."

"And the baby?" my mother asked. "Where is she?"

For a moment I wanted to lie and say there was no baby, but I told myself a queen would never lie. "She's in the kitchen." I motioned to the door with my chin. "Probably asleep."

"May we see her?"

"Sure." I left reluctantly and went to get Nette. She wasn't asleep, and was all smiles when I walked in the door and picked her up from the blanket on the floor.

"Come on, little queen," I said. "You've got some grandparents to meet. Try and be polite now."

I held the baby close as I presented her to my parents, not offering her to them.

"She's beautiful!" My mother reached out a finger for Nette to grab.

"I think so," I said. Then I added, just to see how they would react, "I think she looks a lot like Antoine."

My father's face tightened, and it appeared as if a mask had suddenly covered it. My mother's eyes watered and she looked away. It seemed that they still had not come to terms with Antoine's death.

"Don't, Ari," my mother said.

"My name isn't Ari anymore. It's Ariana," I said bitterly. "You have both buried Ari as surely as you buried Antoine! But you still won't talk about it, will you? Why are you even here? Did you decide that since your beloved son is gone, I will finally have to do?"

Neither of them spoke for what seemed like long minutes. Finally, my father coughed and began. "We wanted to see if you needed help with the baby. Your husband said money was tight, and we thought that if you needed us to, we could take care of her for you, to make sure she had everything she needed."

That made me furious. "Everything material, you mean! Why, Father, I do believe that is the longest thing you've said to me since Antoine's death—except to bawl me out about drinking. What you don't seem to realize is that Nette has everything she needs with me. I love her as you two never loved me! I'm in school, and I'm going to make something of our lives. And I'm never going to make my daughter feel as if she's a half-brained idiot just because she's a girl! No, I can raise my daughter alone, thank you very much! We don't need you, and we don't need your money! Do you know where the last money you gave to Jacques went? Well, I don't know exactly, because he left me the day you gave it to him. But you can be absolutely sure he's on a heroin trip or something worse. That's where your precious money went!" I glared at them defiantly, daring them to deny what I had said.

My father only shook his head. "We shouldn't have come. I can see that you are just as unreasonable as before."

"Me, unreasonable!" I exclaimed, feeling my heart harden even further against them. "You are the ones who come in here thinking that you can rescue my daughter from her horrible situation. Just what makes you think you can raise her better than I can? You don't exactly have a good track record with raising daughters. Even now, you can't admit you are partly at fault for what happened to me after your precious Antoine died!" I was practically screaming at them now, and nearly everyone in the cafe had stopped eating to listen. But I didn't care.

"You left me all alone! Both of you! When Antoine died, part of me died as well. Don't you see? He'd been with me since the moment we were conceived, so in a way he *was* me, because I had never learned to be myself!" I took a deep, shaky breath and said more calmly, "I think you should go now."

My mother was crying openly, and my father put an arm around her to lead her out the door. *At least they seemed to be closer than they were when I left home,* I thought dispassionately.

As I watched them leave, I whispered to Nette, "I sure didn't do too well, did I? I guess acting like a queen takes more practice than I thought." I turned and went into the kitchen where Marguerite was waiting.

"Well?" she asked, as if she hadn't heard practically the whole conversation.

"They wanted Nette," I said sadly, cuddling the baby to me. "They still don't want me."

Marguerite put her arms around my shoulders. "Maybe it just seems so, Ariana. Maybe they simply don't know how to show you they care."

But I didn't believe her.

CHAPTER SEVEN

School came as a wonderful surprise for me. I had never had much interest in learning before, but now I lost myself in the various texts, especially anything to do with mathematics. Equations seemed to practically solve themselves on the page, and I delighted in my newfound talent—one I had never expected. I wondered that I hadn't noticed it before. Maybe it was because for the first time in my life, I was serious about making a career for myself—and, most importantly, a good life for little Nette.

The days, weeks, and months slipped by as I immersed myself in work, school, and my daughter. On the few occasions when I had to take tests, either Marguerite or my next-door neighbor, Jeanne, a mother of two young children herself, would baby-sit Nette.

I was strangely happy and content with most of my life, though I was alone with only Nette for company most of my free time. I hadn't seen any of the gang except for Paulette, who came in regularly in the afternoons during the rush to play with Nette in the kitchen. During these times she was mostly sober and clear-headed, though I knew she was still using many different drugs. But since she never asked to take Nette anywhere and they seemed to delight in each other's company, I let her come.

"Do you miss him?" Paulette asked me one afternoon after the lunch rush, when Nette had just turned eight months old. We were sitting on the floor on a large blanket, eating a late lunch. I had my back propped against the door to the small office, with Nette curled up in my lap, nursing. While she did eat some solid foods, she was late getting teeth and was still dependent upon me for most of her nourishment. Since breast milk was the healthiest—not to mention the cheapest—food available, and because nursing enhanced our closeness, I didn't mind.

"Do I miss him?" I repeated Paulette's question while I seriously thought about it. I didn't have to ask who "him" was. "Well, yes, I guess I do. I miss the way he used to look at me with his head cocked back, as if wanting to catch every word. I miss feeling him in the bed beside me at night, and seeing his tousled hair in the morning. And I miss seeing him play with Nette." I felt the tears forming in my eyes, and I blinked furiously and purposely made my voice hard. "But I don't miss the uncertainty of life with him, the drugs, or the alcohol."

"Would you take him back?" Paulette picked up her sandwich and took a halfhearted bite. Drugs had a way of taking away her appetite. "I mean, if he just showed up one day," she said a trifle unclearly as she chewed.

I took a bite of my own sandwich before I answered, holding it with the hand that wasn't supporting Nette. "I guess that would depend. I mean, I'm not willing to go back to what was before. I'm stable now and working toward a goal, and if I'm not completely happy, well, it's still much better than what life was with him."

"But what if he had changed?"

I snorted. "I don't know if I could believe him—he's lied to me so many times before!" I sighed. "I guess I would probably give him time to prove himself, though I wouldn't hold any great hopes in the matter."

For once, Paulette looked directly into my eyes. "You still love him, don't you?"

I wanted to deny it but found I couldn't. "Yes," I admitted reluctantly. "But I don't want to. And I don't hold any hopes of his coming back changed. He's chosen a different way of life, and that's that."

"I'm not sure I believe it. I think he really loved you."

I shrugged. "'Loved' is the key word here, Paulette. It's past tense. I think it's time I filed for divorce." As I said it, I became determined. It would probably take a good chunk of my savings, but it was a necessary step. I had to cut ties with my unhappy past. I should have done it long ago.

My conversation with Paulette spurred me to action. I went to see several lawyers about my divorce during the next few days. Thursday morning, two days after our talk, I chose one—not the cheapest, but the one I felt would get the job done the fastest. I didn't anticipate any problems from Jacques.

I arrived at work that afternoon feeling a little more depressed than normal, but firm in my decision. I found Marguerite busily showing another woman around the kitchen. She looked much like Marguerite herself, yet fatter and more disapproving and stern.

"Oh, Ariana, come meet my sister, Françoise!" Marguerite motioned to me. As I approached, she scooped the giggling Nette out of my arms to hug and kiss her. "How are you today, precious? Boy, am I going to miss you while I'm on vacation!"

I started at her words. I had completely forgotten that Marguerite and Jules were leaving the next Monday for a month of well-deserved vacation. Her sister and her niece had come to take their places while they were gone, as they had done in other years.

"It's nice to meet you, Françoise," I said, kissing the woman's cheeks several times in the French custom.

"And you, Ariana," Françoise rejoined with a tight smile. Her rolls of fat jiggled as she shifted into a more comfortable position. "I've heard quite a bit about you from Marguerite."

"Oh, Ariana here is a wonder!" Marguerite exclaimed. "Everything is pretty much the same as the other times you came, Françoise, but if you have any problems, just ask Ariana. She knows the job better than I do. And don't worry about little Nette here, she's an absolute angel. We block off part of the kitchen with crates to keep her away from the stove, and she just plays all day. Your daughter Colette will probably love her." Marguerite turned to me. "You'll meet Colette on Monday. She's getting married next spring, you know."

I hadn't known, but nodded anyway. Then Marguerite was off again, reacquainting the corpulent Françoise with the cafe. I stared out the large window and sighed. I wasn't looking forward to life without Marguerite and Jules, even if only for a month, but they certainly had chosen a perfect time to go—the last week of August and the first three of September. I wished I could go with them, but I had tests the next week and they needed me here at the cafe. Still, maybe when they got back, Nette and I would go somewhere really special for our own little vacation. Not somewhere costly, but where we could be alone for a few days and relax from all the pressures of work and school.

The next morning, the day after I paid the lawyer, I got up early for a test. After this one, I would have to take only two more the following week to graduate. I had no doubt that I would pass; I had done nothing more than study every morning for the last four months.

I readied Nette to take to my neighbor, Jeanne, to be baby-sat. Since Marguerite was busy packing for her vacation, she would not be able to sit with her. Nette actually preferred going to Jeanne's because she loved playing with her children. I had often gone there in the mornings during studying breaks to let them play together, especially when I had realized that Marguerite wouldn't always be able to watch Nette during my exams. I hadn't wanted Nette to cry when I left her with Jeanne.

The doorbell rang suddenly, and I ran to answer it.

"Hi, Ariana."

I gasped, feeling my eyes widen as I saw Jacques standing there. I had been so certain I would never see him again, that he was out of my life forever. I almost couldn't believe my eyes.

"Why are you here?" I asked abruptly, holding a hand up to still my heavily beating heart.

He was leaning against the door frame gazing down at me, his head cocked slightly to one side. His eyes were clear and seemingly drug free, although I knew I could not trust myself on this. I had been fooled before.

"I came to see you, Ariana." His voice was soft. "I've missed you terribly."

I steeled myself against the ache in his voice. "I've filed for divorce," I said determinedly.

Jacques frowned and then sighed. "Well, I guess I should have expected as much. Still, it's not final yet. Could you give me another chance?"

"But I don't want to be hurt again, Jacques!" I blurted out. "I can't trust you!"

"I won't hurt you, I promise!"

"Your promises haven't been very good," I pointed out.

He grimaced. "That was five months ago, Ariana. I've changed." His voice was pleading. "Please, just think about it."

I didn't say anything but stared at the ground, trying for all I was worth to avoid looking at the face of the man I knew I still loved. Simply seeing him made my emotions race crazily, compelling me to throw myself into his arms. During the ensuing silence, Nette crawled over from near the couch where I had left her. She stood up, using my legs to steady herself.

"Why, she's so big!" Jacques exclaimed. "Is she walking already?"

"Not alone." I smiled down at the chubby baby. "But it won't be long now. She walks along anything she can hold on to. Most babies don't walk until they're around eleven months. Nette's just extra determined."

"Like her mother," Jacques commented. He knelt down and called Nette to him, but she clung to my legs. Undaunted, he continued to play with her until her cherub face crinkled in a smile. He glanced up at me in triumph. "She likes me!" He continued his play. "She looks so much like you with those huge round eyes and dark hair." He touched his own dark-blond locks with a finger. "Doesn't look much like her dad, that's for sure. And a good thing, too."

"Nonsense, Jacques. You've got brown eyes too, and look at the dimple in her chin—it looks just like yours." I crouched down to point it out to him. Little Nette giggled. She had taken hold of Jacques' fingers and actually took a step in his direction.

"She needs a father," Jacques said suddenly, looking deep into my eyes. "Please, give us another chance!"

I suspected he was using Nette to get to me, but I knew I wanted to try again anyway. "Okay," I agreed. "You can come and see us, and we'll see where things go. But you can't stay here."

Disappointment flared briefly in his eyes, but he seemed willing to live with my rules. "I'll show you, Ariana," he said sincerely. "I still love you, and I know that you love me too."

I shrugged. "I've learned that love isn't everything, Jacques. It doesn't pay the rent, and it is useless without trust."

"Things are going to be different now. You'll see."

I sighed. "Yes, I guess I will. But for now, I've got a test to take." I gathered up my school supplies and slung Nette's diaper bag over my shoulder. "Come on, Nette." I picked up the baby in my free arm and motioned to Jacques to shut the door and to see that it was locked. We started off down the hall towards Jeanne's. At her door, I rang the bell.

She answered almost immediately, flanked by her two toddlers. "Why, good morning!" she sang cheerily. "Do you want to play, Nette?" She held out her arms to take the baby, but Nette kicked to get down with the other children.

"It shouldn't take more than a couple of hours," I said.

Jeanne smiled. "Take whatever time you need." She peered behind me at Jacques and added teasingly, "Who's this handsome guy?"

I grimaced slightly and replied, "This is Nette's father, Jacques. He came to visit this morning, but he's just leaving."

"It's nice to meet you, Jeanne." Jacques held out his hand and smiled his most charming grin. Jeanne practically blushed, and I wanted to roll my eyes in disbelief. Instead, I changed the subject.

"Thanks so much for watching Nette, Jeanne. Will you still be able to watch her Thursday evening?" I had two tests left, and since one was offered only at night, I had decided to take them both Thursday night, one right after the other. That way I wouldn't have to find a baby-sitter again.

"It's no bother, really," Jeanne said. "And Thursday's fine. Did you get time off at the cafe?"

"Yes, I traded for Monday." I glanced at my watch. "Goodness, I've got to get down to the school or I'll miss my test!" I reached to give Nette a final kiss and then ran to the elevator. Jacques followed me down the hall.

"I could have watched her," he said as we waited.

I snorted incredulously. "She doesn't even know you! And there's still that little matter of trust. Don't push it, Jacques."

"Okay," he agreed hastily. "But can I walk you to wherever you're going?"

"Sure, if you can keep up."

The next few days, Jacques seemed to be everywhere I turned. That first day, he waited for me after my test, walked back with me to get Nette, and stayed until I went to work. Later, he came back to eat dinner at the cafe, then came back again to wait for me outside after I closed up.

"You don't have to walk me home, Jacques," I said, pointing to the apartment building door that stood five paces down from the cafe. "I'm quite safe as long as I check the streets before I make a run for it."

"But I want to, Ariana." He pointed to the sleeping baby. "May I carry her for you?"

"Sure." It had been a long day, and I was happy to let him do some of the work for a change. I unlocked the outer apartment door and held it open for him. Then I went in myself, turning to make sure the heavy door clicked shut behind us.

Once in the apartment, Jacques carried Nette to my recently-purchased bed. "You've got a nice place here," he said as he looked around the room.

"I've been working hard," I said softly.

His face darkened slightly. "I'm sorry for everything before, Ariana. I really am. I want to be the man that you want and need—and love."

"Let's take one day at a time, Jacques. But now I'm really tired, and I've still got to work all day tomorrow."

"What about in the morning? We could walk along the river like we used to."

I smiled. "Okay, Jacques."

After he left, hope and fear wrestled within me until I was too tired to think. At last I fell asleep, cuddled to the warmth of Nette's tiny body.

CHAPTER EIGHT

Saturday morning dawned bright and shining, giving more than a hint of the heat to come later in the day. Jacques came as promised, still clear-eyed and hopeful, and we spent a wonderful morning together. Little Nette warmed up even more toward him; it was as if she somehow remembered him from before.

We walked along the river, and once again I showed Nette the Palais de Justice and told her the story of Queen Marie-Antoinette. She laughed and babbled back to me as she always did, not understanding anything except the love in my voice.

"Your daughter is going to be a queen, did you know, Jacques?" I said, smiling and looking tenderly at Nette.

He returned my smile with a grin. "She already is. Just like you." I wanted to tell him no, that we weren't yet, but he had reached over to kiss my cheek, sending chills throughout my body.

We made our way back to the cafe, and Jacques stayed for lunch. He came back later for dinner and to walk us home. He was trying his best to be charming and considerate, and I couldn't help the feelings of love that arose in my heart.

"What about tomorrow?" he asked. "Let's spend the day together. You still have Sundays off, don't you? We'll take a picnic and go somewhere or something." He stroked Nette's soft cheek and then reached out to touch mine. A shiver ran through me at his touch, as it had that morning when he kissed me.

"Okay, Jacques. I'd like that."

He quickly tucked Nette into her bed and whirled me around. "You don't worry about food or anything," he said excitedly. "I'll take care of it all!" He kissed me once, hard, on the mouth. "I love you, Ariana de Cotte!" He was out the door and gone before I could say another word.

I suddenly wanted things to work out desperately. It was difficult and sometimes very lonely raising a child alone. How much easier it would be with a husband to share the responsibilities!

I was dressed and waiting Sunday morning when Jacques showed up at ten with a huge basket filled to brimming with different foods. He kissed me on the cheek and turned to hug little Nette. This time she didn't pull away. On the way to the elevator, we passed my neighbor Jeanne in the hall. "Good morning, pretty lady," Jacques said with a winning smile.

Jeanne laughed. "You've got yourself a charming one there!" she said to me.

"You can say that again!"

We were quiet on the ride down the elevator and out into the street. Jacques headed purposely toward a waiting taxi. "Where are we going?" I asked.

He grinned. "It's a secret, just wait and see. But I'm sure you'll enjoy it."

We sat in comfortable silence as the taxi careened through Paris, ever conscious of the driver and his interested stare. Soon we reached the city's outskirts where there was a beautiful, green countryside so unlike the crowded city that I had almost forgotten such things existed. It had been too long since I had visited similar places—since Antoine died. "Oh, this is beautiful, Jacques!" I exclaimed, breathing deep the fresh air.

Jacques looked so happy he could burst. "You go on ahead, honey, and I'll arrange with the taxi driver to come back for us later."

I went on ahead and found a calm, shady spot under a tree and out of sight of the narrow road. Nette laughed in delight and immediately tried to eat the dirt. I laughed until I choked while Nette eyed me curiously, as if trying to figure out what had overcome her mother.

The day was inconceivably perfect. Jacques was so wonderful—so normal and caring. I thought that all my dreams had finally come true. The only damper on the whole day turned out to be from Nette. When time came for her nap, she refused to sleep and cried and cried. The only thing that made her feel better was to nurse, but she soon became full and cried because there was too much milk. "What's wrong with her?" Jacques asked, looking as frustrated as I felt. I knew he'd been hoping for some romantic time alone that Nette's nap would have allowed us.

I shook my head. "I don't know; she rarely does this. It could be that she's finally teething. Marguerite says it's quite painful for some babies."

"Don't you have anything to give her?"

"At home I do. But she's never needed it. I certainly wasn't expecting her to do this today."

Jacques sighed. "We could give her some of this wine." He motioned to the half-empty bottle in the picnic basket. I shook my head vigorously. He sighed again and put the bottle back into the basket. "Well, the taxi driver won't be back for an hour yet."

"Then let's go for a walk," I suggested. "Maybe she'll calm down."

"It's worth a try," Jacques agreed, jumping up.

I carried the whimpering Nette in my arms and followed him down a small path. The trees still hid us from the mid-afternoon sun, making the heat tolerable and even pleasant. It was beautiful there, but I found it hard to enjoy through Nette's cries. Occasionally Jacques cast a worried glance at us, holding stray branches back so that I wouldn't have to duck or push them away to pass.

We had walked only a short way when we spied a small stream. Immediately, I made for the water. "This ought to do it." I took off Nette's shoes and socks and my own and put our feet into the water. Nette stopped whining abruptly and stared, fascinated, at the stream. It was all I could do to keep her from plunging in altogether.

Jacques and I relaxed and sat with our feet in the water, talking quietly. The area was peaceful and undisturbed, the silence broken only by our voices, the birds chirping, or the unhurried movement of the little stream. We seemed to be the only three people in the whole world. But eventually the taxi driver came and we went home, listening to Nette's renewed screams nearly the whole way. At our apartment, I found the teething remedy and immediately gave it to her. She screamed for another half hour, nursed again, and finally fell asleep. With a sigh of relief, I put her into bed.

"Whew! I didn't know she could be like that," Jacques said.

I laughed. "Neither did I. She's full of surprises, that's for sure." I sat down on the couch and laid my head back, exhausted.

Jacques sat down beside me. "You still have Mondays off?" he asked hopefully.

"Normally I do. But Marguerite is leaving on vacation, and she wanted me to be there the first few days to make sure her sister and niece can manage without me. So this week I agreed to trade for Thursday. It works out so that I can take my tests."

"What about in the morning?"

I shook my head. "No, I've got to study, Jacques, really I do. It's very important to me."

"But I'm back now, and I'm going to take care of you."

I sat up stiffly. "Oh, Jacques, that has nothing to do with my going to school! I like school, and I want to finish. Plus, I'm going to take a college accounting program in January so I can get a job at a bank or someplace when Nette is old enough for school. That way I can be here for her when she comes home. But it's something I want to do for myself, as well as for her."

"But you can stay home all you want now, because money's not an issue anymore," Jacques insisted.

"Did you suddenly get a job that pays millions?" I asked, a little angry. He didn't seem to understand that I *wanted* to go to school.

"Not quite, but I make about ten times what I used to."

I regarded him suspiciously. *Could this be another one of his lies?* I thought. Aloud I said, "What do you do, Jacques?"

"I'm self-employed," he said.

That made me wonder even more. "Doing what?"

He shrugged. "Nothing out of the ordinary. I sell things door-to-door. And I have people who work for me." He moved closer and put his arm around my shoulders. "But the point is that I can get you anything you want now, even a bigger apartment. With room enough for the three of us." He leaned over and nibbled on my ear.

For the first time, I noticed Jacques was wearing clothes of the finest make, similar to the clothes I had been accustomed to when I had lived with my parents—clothes I now saved for special occasions like school, doctor's appointments, or college registration. I glanced down at my own worn jeans. Could he be telling the truth? I wanted to believe in him, but I was so afraid. I needed time to think.

I pulled away. "I need time, Jacques. I—I'm still not certain things will be different than the last time. Give me time, please?"

He studied me for a minute and then nodded once, sharply. "Okay, we'll leave it for now, Ariana. But I will win out, you'll see." He stood up, leaned down to kiss my forehead, and made his way slowly to the door. "I'll be by again. See ya."

After he left, I went about straightening the apartment and getting Nette's bag ready for the next day. As I set it by the door where I wouldn't forget, I noticed that my extra set of keys was not on the hook near the door. I wondered briefly if I had put them in my purse, or perhaps given them to Nette to play with as I sometimes did. But tiredness overwhelmed me and I shrugged the matter aside. They would turn up eventually.

On Monday I didn't see Jacques at all. It was a normal day for me, yet I longed for the light and love his presence had brought back into my life. Work at the cafe went smoothly and efficiently under the firm control of the massive Françoise. I didn't take to the woman, but I readily liked her daughter, Colette, who at twenty-one was two years my senior.

"She is so beautiful!" Colette had exclaimed the minute she caught sight of Nette. She eyed me up and down. "And looking at you, I can see why. I wish I had smaller bones. But, alas! I inherited my mother's strong ones. Oh, well, I guess I'll make do." She sighed dramatically, and her mother rolled her eyes. I laughed. Colette wasn't lying when she said she had large bones, but she was fairly pretty, regardless.

That night after work, a strange depression settled upon me. I knew then that I had been hoping to see Jacques. Nette's sleeping form felt heavier than usual, and I wished he were there to carry her to my apartment. Like the day before on our picnic, she had cried and cried all day at the cafe. I was sure she was teething because her gums were red and sore-looking. I had given her two more doses of the pain remedy, and it had helped a little. Not for the first time, though, I wished I didn't have to work at the cafe at all but could stay home and take care of my baby properly. I was so tired.

Nothing felt different than usual when I put my key into the lock of my apartment. But when I opened it, I immediately saw the difference and gasped. At first I was so shocked that I wondered if somehow I had entered the wrong apartment by mistake.

The entire room was filled with my favorite flowers—pure white roses. There were vases and more vases of them in all sizes and shapes. On the short coffee table in front of the sofa stood a large vase with two dozen long-stemmed roses of the darkest red, and a small note.

I went to put Nette down in the bedroom, where more roses adorned my dresser and even the floor. A quick scan around the apartment showed that the kitchen and even the bathroom held more of the flawless white roses. I returned to the living room and sat down on the sofa to read the short note: "To Ariana with love, Jacques."

Suddenly, I knew what had happened to my other set of keys.

I sat speechless, looking around the room in amazement. This was every young girl's dream; but I was no longer a girl, though I was still young. I was a mother first, and an impoverished one at that. Instead of enjoying them and basking in the love with which they had been given, I swiftly calculated that the roses cost more than two months' rent, which I actually could have used a lot more. That made me laugh. Still, if Jacques could waste money like this, maybe he *had* changed.

The next day I gave some of the roses to Jeanne, telling her what Jacques had done. "You should hang on to that one," she said laughingly.

"We'll see." I wasn't quite so ready to trust him yet.

I also took some of the flowers to the cafe, where I worked halfheartedly, hoping Jacques would visit me. He came in shortly after noon, wearing dark sunglasses. Two rich-looking gentlemen were with him. "Hi, honey," he said. "I wanted to come and see you earlier, but I've been working." He motioned over his shoulder to the men. "These are some of my . . . clients. Could you get us the best meal you've got and bring it to the table? These guys are used to posher places, but I wanted to come and see you." He counted out various bills and laid them on the counter. "And keep the change, love."

I tried not to show my surprise. The "change" would be more than half the money he had given me. "Keep it for Nette," Jacques urged when he saw that I was going to refuse.

That made sense. He was, after all, her father. "For Nette," I said. "And thank you for the roses, though it was way too much, Jacques."

He grinned. "Nothing's too much for you, Ariana." I wished his eyes were uncovered so that I could see his expression, but the glasses hid them well. I couldn't help the dark suspicion that he was hiding something from me—and perhaps from his clients as well.

I smiled anyway and motioned him to the corner table. "Sit down, and I'll bring it out to you." I rang up the special order and then slipped into the kitchen to give it to Colette. I stopped briefly to kiss and hug little Nette, who was deeply involved in playing with a set of spoons that Colette had given her to play with. Beside her on the blanket, Paulette was trying unsuccessfully to build a tepee with some of the spoons.

I tucked Jacques' extra money into the diaper bag. "That's from your daddy, Nette. It sure is easy to act like a queen when that's how you're treated." The baby grinned, her mouth opening to show the sliver of a tooth that had nearly broken through. For the moment, she seemed to be free of pain and content. I hoped she stayed that way. But at least Paulette would be there to help for a while if she did start screaming.

When I got back to the counter, the lunch rush began in earnest. I worked feverishly to clear the customers so I would be free to take the food to Jacques' table. But people kept coming, and when Colette was finished with their plates, I couldn't get free. Françoise was also very busy and couldn't take my place at the register. I shrugged and motioned for Colette to take the food to Jacques' table, hiding my disappointment. But there would be plenty of time for us later. The rush of people continued for hours, and I didn't even see Jacques when he left or have time to ask him for my keys.

I didn't see him again until the next morning, when he arrived at my apartment door unannounced. Like the previous day, he had his dark glasses on.

"Come in," I invited. "Care for some orange juice?"

Jacques shook his head. "I've got to run. Business, you know. I just wanted to come by and give my girls a kiss." He kissed me quickly on the lips and reached down for Nette.

"Mamma," Nette gurgled.

"No, I'm your daddy, silly girl." Jacques kissed her and Nette smiled. "Hey, she's getting a tooth!"

I nodded. "And more coming. I hope she doesn't keep being so ornery. At least yesterday I had a rest, though. She was an angel." As I spoke, Nette reached up to firmly grasp Jacques' glasses and pulled them off before he could stop her. My heart pounded furiously as I instantly saw what Jacques had been hiding. He was still using drugs.

Jacques shoved the glasses on again quickly as if nothing had happened. He gave Nette another kiss and handed her to me. "Well, I'll see ya. Have a good day. I'll come by tonight." He left and I stood in the doorway, watching him go. At the same time, Jeanne and her two children left their apartment. They entered the elevator with Jacques, laughing and talking.

I shut the door slowly. Nothing had changed, not really. As long as he was using drugs, things would be exactly as they had been before. Eventually he would lose or give up even this latest job that seemed so lucrative.

Tears came rapidly as I slid down to the floor with my back pressed against the closed door, arms tightly wrapped around my innocent baby.

"I wish he hadn't come back," I told Paulette later that afternoon. I wanted to strangle Jacques for giving me hope and then failing to live up to my expectations. To make things worse, Nette had been screaming constantly almost all day. The only time she even stopped for a breath was when I was holding her. I had given her the baby medicine to no avail, and had finally strapped her to my chest until Paulette had shown up sometime after the lunch rush was ended. My back and legs ached, and I felt miserable.

"Hey, at least he can give you some money to help out with Nette," Paulette said.

"But what about me?"

Paulette shrugged. "He isn't good enough for you. You're special, Ariana. Even I know that."

"I don't want to be special, Paulette. I just want to have someone to depend on."

But it seemed I couldn't depend on Jacques, even to come and see me when he said he would. That night I had planned to tell him it was over between us, but he didn't show up at the apartment. Nette screamed for hours before we both finally fell asleep on the couch, exhausted. In the morning, I awoke to find Nette nursing. I didn't remember pulling up my nightshirt, but there she was, gulping down milk as if there wasn't going to be any later on. She appeared rested despite the horrible night and smiled up at me as I looked at her, losing the nipple for her efforts. She stopped smiling and sucked with renewed energy. I smiled back at her and tried to stretch my stiff body. My neck ached from sleeping on the couch, and my back was still sore from carrying Nette in the carrier. I sighed. At least I didn't have to go to work. Today was Thursday, the day I would finish school.

I took the morning easy, not even opening a book until I got Nette to sleep after lunch. She was cranky but tired, and fell asleep quickly. I was relieved because I had used the rest of the pain medicine the night before. After she dozed off, I reviewed the test material, but I already knew it well and found my mind wandering. Soon, I too was fast asleep.

Hours later, we awoke together. I nursed Nette again and got her ready to take to Jeanne's house. "It's only for a little while," I chattered to Nette nervously. "And when you see me again, I'll be a graduate—or near enough, anyway." I hugged her and covered her face with kisses until she laughed with delight. "Oh, I love you so much, Nette," I whispered against her cheek. "And no matter what, I wouldn't take back a second of my life if that meant I wouldn't have you."

I glanced at the clock and saw that it was time to go.

"I hope she doesn't scream for you, Jeanne," I said as I dropped the baby off. "I ran out of that baby medicine, but I fell asleep after lunch and didn't have time to buy any more."

"That's okay, I have some if it's needed. And I'm used to babies crying. Just go on and do a good job on your test."

"Thanks, Jeanne. I don't know what I'd do without you."

"Well, you'd manage somehow, I'm sure. Besides, it doesn't seem as though you'll be needing me for long, with that handsome husband of yours back in the picture."

I didn't have time to tell her the truth about Jacques, but I would tell her all about it later when I picked Nette up. As I left the apartment building, warm rain started falling lightly and then more quickly. By the time I reached the school, I was soaked.

The tests were long, but not especially grueling. The first was mathematics, and I flew through it, finishing early. That meant I had to wait an hour to even start the last one. But soon I was on my way back home, anxious to see Nette. It was still raining hard, odd for August but greatly needed by the dry earth. I hurried quickly through the wet streets, trying to avoid the deep puddles on the cobblestone and cement sidewalks, hating the rain for the memories it brought of Antoine's death. The cloudy sky was darker than usual and there was lightning nearby, thunder sounding loud and threatening like a dire warning. My heart began pounding loudly in my chest and in my ears. I started running.

The hall seemed eerily quiet when I arrived at Jeanne's door. For no reason I could define, I felt my heart constrict in fear. I rang the bell quickly. "Hi, Ariana," Jeanne said brightly when she opened the door. "What do you need?"

I blinked. "What do you mean? I came to pick up Nette."

"You did?" She looked at me in surprise. "That's strange. Your husband came to get her hours ago. He said you told him to, and that he was going to take Nette to wait in your apartment. He had your keys and everything. I thought it would be okay, so I let him take her. I even stood here and watched him go into your apartment. Did I do wrong?" she asked anxiously.

"I hope not, Jeanne." But I couldn't stop the horrible worry that clutched my breast or the pressure that had begun in my head. "Did you hear her crying or anything?"

Jeanne nodded. "My husband did. You see, I left to visit my mother for a little while, and when he came home he heard the baby crying. He went to pick me up at my mother's, and when he told me Nette was crying we came right home. But we couldn't hear her crying anymore. I guess she'd fallen asleep." She paused a moment. "I'm sorry if I shouldn't have given Nette to Jacques, but I thought everything was worked out between you two."

"I should have told you," I mumbled and started quickly down the hall. It seemed to take forever to reach my apartment. The door was locked; I shoved the key in and opened it quickly, hoping that everything would be all right.

But I already knew, deep inside, that my world had changed forever.

CHAPTER NINE

Paulette sat stiffly on my couch. Her dark eyes were large and frightened as she looked at me, tears rolling down her cheeks.

"What is it, Paulette?" I asked, my voice sharp with worry. I glanced around the apartment. Used cups and plates littered the floor and coffee table. Food was ground into the nice carpet. It appeared as if someone had thrown a wild party. "Tell me!" My voice was beginning to sound hysterical. I ran to the bedroom, frantically searching for my baby. "Nette? Where are you, Nette? Come to Mommy!" But she was nowhere to be found.

I ran over to Paulette and shook her. "Where is my baby? Did Jacques take her?"

Paulette shook her head almost violently. "No, not like that. He wanted to surprise you, to show you that he could take care of Nette. But she kept crying, so he went to the cafe and called me down at the bar. He was pretty upset and mumbling about how he was going to get a phone installed here, and how there was no one home next door, and how he couldn't find the baby medicine. I could hear Nette crying over the phone, and some of the guys and I came to see if we could help. I played with her like I do at the cafe, but she just kept crying and crying and chewing on her fist." Paulette bit her lip as the tears came faster. "Jacques couldn't stand seeing her in pain, and he wasn't thinking right. None of us were. We'd all been shooting up and stuff. Jacques had given us a lot of free stuff. He's been dealing, you know, though I only found out last night or I would have told you before."

I shook her again. "Paulette, my baby! Tell me about my baby!"

Paulette gazed at me sorrowfully. "Jacques shot a little bit of stuff into her. You know, just a little, to try and get her to calm down—"

"No! He didn't!" I shook my head incredulously. *Could anyone be so stupid as to give drugs to a baby?*

Paulette gulped. "She calmed down after that and seemed happy. She went to sleep and everyone began to celebrate. But I was worried about Nette, so I kept checking on her. And then once she wasn't breathing, and I told Jacques. He gave her mouth-to-mouth and she started breathing again, but she didn't wake up. Jacques got real scared and took her to the hospital."

"Is she all right?" I demanded, holding my breath for the answer.

"I don't know!" Paulette wailed tearfully. "It's all my fault, Ariana! I shouldn't have let it happen!" She bit her lip again until a trickle of blood appeared. The pain seemed to help her concentrate. "After Jacques left, I went and called the police and they sent someone to the hospital. I told them I'd come back and wait for you here, and we'd meet them down there. I'm so sorry, Ariana!"

I was out the door before she finished talking. I didn't wait for the elevator, but shot down the stairs and into the stormy night, running for all I was worth. Paulette followed behind me, trying to keep up.

Jacques was pacing the hospital halls when I arrived. If he had been drugged before—and I didn't doubt that he had—all traces were blotted out by the stark realization of what he had done. Nearby, two policemen waited to take Jacques to the police station after Nette's condition was known.

I ran to the desk, tears blocking my vision. "My baby, how is she?"

The nurse didn't ask who I was, she just shook her head gently. "I don't know. The doctor should be out as soon as he knows."

I waited there with my heart aching, hardly believing that such a thing could actually be happening. Surely this was a nightmare, and I would soon wake up. I shook myself repeatedly, but it seemed this nightmare was real.

Jacques came close to me, his face lit eerily by the fluorescent lights of the hospital. "I'm sorry," he said. His were eyes pleading, begging for absolution. "It seemed the right thing to do at the time. She was in pain."

I turned on him in contempt. "And what about now, Jacques? What kind of pain is she in now? Oh, I wish you had never come back! We were happy without you. Why couldn't you just leave us alone?" I retreated from him, backing down the orange carpet that contrasted so harshly with the stark white walls. Jacques started to follow me, but I held up a hand to motion him back. "Stay away from me!" I ordered. Defeated, Jacques stayed where he was.

The doctor came out minutes later. The nurse at the desk quickly guided him over to me. "This is the baby's mother," she said softly.

The doctor looked at me gravely. "I'm sorry," he said. "Her body couldn't handle that amount of drugs in her system."

"No!" I whispered. "No!" The doctor and his words seemed unreal. I stared at him, noticing the short hairs growing stiffly out from his face as if he hadn't had time to shave that day.

"If it helps to know," he said kindly, "she didn't feel any pain at all. She just went to sleep."

My heart ached so badly that I thought I would die. "Can I see her?" I asked hoarsely, not bothering to wipe away the tears that were streaming down my face.

He nodded. "Of course. Come with me." We turned to go through the door, but Jacques put his arm out to stop me.

"Please, Ariana!" he sobbed. "I didn't mean it!"

Anger swept over me like a fire raging out of control. "I don't care what you say!" I hissed at him. "Nothing can change the fact that you murdered our baby—the only person alive that means anything to me! You are a murderer, and I hope you rot in hell forever!" I hoped the words burned into his soul as severely as his action had destroyed mine.

His face was stricken. "Ariana, I—" But I turned and followed the doctor. Out of the corner of my eye I saw the policemen leading Jacques down the orange carpet, a broken parody of the man I once loved.

The doctor led me to a room crowded with equipment. In the center was a large table with a still figure on it, seeming small and lost in the midst of a huge expanse of white. Nette looked as though she were asleep, so perfect and angelic. At any moment, I expected her to open her eyes and smile at me. Strangely, I felt her presence in the room, though I knew she was dead. I touched her white cheek softly and then picked up her limp body and cuddled her to my chest. Already, my milk was letting down in anticipation of the baby that would never nurse again.

"Oh, Antoinette," I whispered. "I should never have left you. I'm so sorry. Now you will never grow up—but you will always be my little queen." As I said her name, I remembered Antoine and how he had also died during a rainstorm nearly two years before. I also thought of Queen Marie-Antoinette and how she had been beheaded. "I shouldn't have named you Antoinette," I sobbed suddenly, sinking into a nearby chair. "People with that name never live very long."

I don't know how much time passed as I sat there, holding my precious baby close to me. Eventually the doctor took her, and I let her go because the essence that had been Nette was no longer in the little body. The presence I had felt in the room had also gone; Nette was lost to me forever.

I stood to go home, but found my strength waning. I made it as far as the waiting room before I sank onto one of the brown couches in a haze of inner pain.

"Ariana." I looked up to see a young woman in a nurse's uniform. Somehow she seemed very familiar to me. "It's Monique. We had the same dance class in school when we were children."

I stared at her dumbly, wondering what difference that fact could possibly make to me. But uninvited, the memories came flooding back. She belonged to the happy times when Antoine had been alive, and those times were gone and better forgotten.

"I was with your baby from the time she came in tonight," she added softly. "I left when you came in to see her. You didn't notice me, and I wanted you to have time with her alone, so I didn't say anything." She had tears in her eyes. "I just wanted you to know how sorry I was. It's horrible to see these things happen, even though I know the children go straight to heaven."

"There is no heaven," I replied dully. "She's dead, and that's all there is." I got up quickly and went out into the rainy night, leaving Monique to stare after me. I didn't want the stranger she'd become to see my pain. Besides, I knew deep inside that the accident was my fault, that somehow I deserved what had happened. I kept seeing little Nette's face before me, crying in Jacques' arms, wondering where her mother was. I had failed her miserably.

The rain had lessened while I was in the hospital. The drops still came down, but only halfheartedly. I made my way slowly, almost blindly, to the metro. It was very dark and I saw no one in the street. The hospital district seemed quiet and peaceful in the early morning, as if denying the innocent death that had occurred. The narrow roads and sidewalks were full of large puddles, but I apathetically sloshed through them; it was too much effort to go around.

A revving car sounded in the distance and soon came careening into sight around a corner. The windows were open and I could hear the laughter of young teenagers, yet unburdened by the sorrows of life and death. They came down the street at an incredible pace, then swerved purposely into the deep puddle at the edge of the street. They laughed with renewed glee as the dirty water flew up to completely soak me. Abruptly they were gone and I went on, barely noticing or caring about the indignity. What difference could a little dirty water make when my baby was dead?

I made it home somehow, though I remembered little of the trip. I didn't turn on the lights in my apartment, but sat on the couch in the darkness, clutching my daughter's white stuffed bear, the one I had bought her the day after Jacques had left us, and feeling my breasts fill with milk until I wondered if they would burst.

I must have dozed off, because the apartment was suddenly bathed in morning light. Still I sat clutching the bear. I got up to use the bathroom sometime later and noticed the roses there. One by one, I pulled the petals from the flowers and let them fall to the tiled floor. Then I did the same to all the other flowers in the apartment, their remains mixing red and white, like blood against pale skin, with the clutter and mess that Jacques' friends had left behind. I felt a tempest of anger inside of me; but worse still was the horrible emptiness in my arms.

And I kept seeing Nette's crying face, calling to me hopelessly.

Several times my doorbell rang, but I didn't answer. I was slumped to the floor in my bedroom, once again clasping Nette's bear to my swollen breasts. Night fell, and still I did not move. My breasts became sore and rocklike. The ache of a breast infection came swiftly after, with alternating chills and fever. But I didn't care; the fever at least gave me some mental relief from the pain in my soul.

The next morning, I heard someone ring the doorbell. This time they didn't go away. A key turned in the lock. "What a mess!" someone said; and then, "Ariana? Are you here? Colette, why don't you check that way, and I'll check back there."

"Oh, I hope she's all right," Colette said. "I knew something was wrong when she didn't show up to work yesterday."

"We've got to find her," replied the other voice that seemed familiar to me, but I couldn't quite place it. "I've even been to her parents', searching, after I came here yesterday and got no answer. But she hasn't been home, and no one has seen her since the hospital."

The voice had moved from the living room to the bathroom and now into my room. At first she didn't see me in a heap on the floor, but then she gasped and ran to my side. I looked up at her almost unseeing. It was Monique from the hospital.

"Colette, she's in here!" Monique cradled me for a moment until Colette came into the room. "Go get my bag, please, and bring a cup of water from the kitchen." Colette quickly obliged.

"How do you feel, Ariana?" Monique asked, but I just shivered.

"What's wrong with her?" Colette's voice was worried.

"Breast infection, I'd guess." She reached out tentatively to touch my left breast. "Yes, it's hard and swollen. She ran out of the hospital before I could get the doctor to give her something to suppress the milk. Now she needs an antibiotic, but I can't get her any if she doesn't go back to the hospital."

That brought a reaction from me. "No, I won't go! Let me be!" I was nearly hysterical as I struggled to get away. If they thought I was going back to that place of nightmares, the place that had taken my baby away, they were crazy.

"So what are we going to do, Monique—carry her?"

Monique shook her head. "She won't die from this; the body has a way of curing itself, and I brought some things to help. An antibiotic would do the job faster, but she's a bit unreasonable right now." Monique's words weren't cruel, they were simply stating a fact.

"Who could blame her?" Colette's voice was rough with sympathy.

Monique began taking items out of her bag. "Vitamin C. She should take a thousand milligrams every hour until she's better. We'll also give her E, at least four of the garlic capsules, and four of these cayenne capsules. We should repeat these dosages every four hours or so."

"How do you know all this?" Colette asked Monique. "I thought most medical people were against all this natural stuff."

Monique smiled. "I think that mostly we medical people are an impatient bunch and just don't like to wait around for nature or the herbs God gave us to take their course. But my grandmother, who raised me, knew all about herbs and vitamins. Many people would come to her for help, and I sort of learned by watching. It's part of why I became a nurse."

As she was talking, Monique had taken the capsules from the bottles and was making me swallow them. I did as she asked, too spent from my previous outburst to protest. Besides, a fiery pain had begun inside my chest, and I couldn't breathe without feeling the agony.

"Now what?" Colette asked.

Monique wrinkled her nose. "A bath, I think. How did you get so dirty, Ariana?" I shrugged indifferently, but as she started to lift me, I fleetingly remembered the youngsters and the dirty water splashing up to soak me. "We've got to get this dirt off," Monique continued. "Then I can put a poultice on your breasts to help you get better."

They helped me into the bath. The hot water felt good and seemed to ease the pain somewhat. Monique found my hand breast pump and made me take some of the milk out of each swollen breast to relieve the pressure. It hurt incredibly, but didn't compare with the suffering in my soul. Afterwards, I lay on the bed while Monique made up the poultice.

"Some slippery elm powder mixed with warm water, add a little comfrey, lobelia and goldenseal, and there you have it." She spread the mixture on two rectangular cloths and made me pull up my nightshirt. Carefully she wrapped them around my reddened breasts and covered them with plastic. "This is to keep it moist. We'll leave it on overnight and see how it does."

"Well, I've got to get down to the cafe," Colette said suddenly. "But I'll be back for a minute every hour or so to check on you, Ariana. And don't worry about the cafe. Mother and I can handle it, and if we can't, we'll find someone to fill in. I'm also calling Marguerite." She reached down to kiss my cheek and tears flooded her eyes. "I'm so sorry about Nette," she whispered. She looked so miserable that I felt I had to say something.

"Thank you for coming, Colette."

She smiled slightly. "I'll be back later." She turned and left the room.

That left Monique and me alone. "Thank you," I murmured and drifted off into oblivion. But even there, I was not freed from the agony in my heart or the throbbing emptiness of my arms.

During the next few days I slowly recovered. At least my body did. Inside I still ached for Nette, and Antoine as well. On the fourth day the fever was completely gone, though I was still weak. Monique was with me, as she had been constantly except for when she had to work at the hospital. She had cleaned the apartment, washed my clothes, and put most of Nette's toys in a box out of sight. Now she was making dinner, singing snatches of different songs as she worked. I mostly just sat and stared into space.

Monique finished adding the final ingredients to her soup and came to where I sat on the couch. She looked at me earnestly. "Oh, Ariana, you're going to make it! I know it doesn't seem as though you will right now, but you will. I know that when my parents . . ." She gulped audibly. "That when my parents died, I thought my life was over. But then there was Grandma, and I found a new life and the gospel of Jesus Christ. It explained the reasons for why everything happened and gave me the strength to go on. And you'll make it, too. You were always so strong, even when we were kids. I admired that in you."

I shook my head. "It wasn't me, it was Antoine."

"No, it was you, Ariana. Antoine had strength too, but you were his source. He loves you so much."

I began to cry at that. "*Loved,* you mean. Don't you know that he's dead?"

She nodded. "I read about it in the paper. I felt bad, because I had run into him a couple of weeks before, and we had met a few times for lunch after that. We had planned to meet again the day after he died, but he never showed up or called. I thought he had dumped me."

"No. Antoine would never have done that to anyone." Her story called up memories I had long forgotten, as I suddenly remembered Antoine telling me about running into the friend from my childhood dance class. He had wanted me to go to with him that last time. But then he died, and—

"Just as you would never have done that to anyone," Monique agreed. "I understood that afterwards, but at the time I didn't know him well enough, though I was crazy about him. I thought I had finally found my Mr. Right, though he was a year younger than me. He was such a good person." She paused a moment and then added, "You and Antoine are a lot alike, you know."

"Well, we are twins. Or were."

That seemed to spark something inside of Monique. "Are! You still *are* twins! Don't you see that this life isn't the end? The body dies, yes, but our spirits are eternal. Don't you believe in God and that he created us? Well, I do. I know that we are his children, and we are as eternal as he is, only we haven't progressed as far. Oh, Ariana, he loves us so much! Don't you think he has a plan to reunite us with our loved ones? He does! I feel it! Please believe that!"

I looked at her, seeing her for the first time. Something she said seemed to speak directly to my soul, to all my treasured hopes hidden deep within. And yet the part of me that hurt so badly was afraid to hope and didn't want any part of it. Abruptly, I saw Nette's beautiful, perfect face as it had been in the hospital. I had felt her then, just for a moment, hadn't I? But the thought that she still existed somewhere brought even more agony to my soul. "Then where is my baby now, Monique?" I asked, feeling my heart breaking all over again. "Who's holding her? Who's singing to her and telling her how much she's loved?"

She gazed at me with understanding. "People often ask me that same question in the hospital," she said quietly. "I personally think that your little Nette is with Antoine. And I think he is holding her and loving her, and telling her all the things you want her to know. He'll watch over her until you are able to be with her again. And knowing she is well taken care of, you can do something meaningful with the time you are apart from her."

Dumbfounded, I stared at her. For the first time since Nette died, I felt myself focusing on something other than my loss and my feelings of guilt and pain. I didn't know exactly where heaven was, but I suddenly wanted to believe in it. I could almost see Antoine holding and kissing Nette. And abruptly I knew what I had to do. Antoine had died for no reason, but Nette's death wouldn't be in vain.

Monique watched my reaction closely. "I have some friends from my church who spend two years out of their lives to teach these things. Wouldn't you like to listen to them?"

I shook my head. "No, Monique. I know what I'm going to do." She regarded me curiously as I continued. "I'm going to make Nette's death mean something. I'm going to call the coalition against drugs that they're always advertising on TV, and I'm going to volunteer. What happened to Nette should never happen to anyone, and I want to make sure no one ever has to go through this hell that I'm living!"

Monique nodded. "That is a definite step in the right direction. I knew you would find a way to come out of this." I nodded, but I think we both knew inside that I was just hiding the pain away so I didn't have to look at it right then, masking the hurt with anger and action. Still, I had survived terrible loss before, and I knew that with time the pain would dim.

After lunch, we went down to the cafe, where I called the drug hotline and told them my story, still so fresh and painful. The woman on the phone seemed very interested and said she'd get back with me after talking to her supervisor. I went back to my apartment, grateful to leave the pitying stares of the cafe customers behind. Again I sat on the couch clutching Nette's bear, staring into nothingness. I didn't notice when Monique left for work.

The next day, two women and a man from the Anti-drug Coalition appeared outside my apartment. They talked with me for hours and finally asked me to be the focus of a new television campaign. I would have to tell parts of my story on camera, and they would use the footage to warn others of the terrible potential of drugs. Posters and personal appearances would also be required. I was overwhelmed with their plans, though grateful for something to focus on. We made a date for the following week to begin working on the campaign. *Somehow,* I told myself, *I will do this.* But the pain in my chest made it so that I could scarcely breathe.

They also planned to attend Nette's burial the next day. "We'll stay in the background," one of the woman promised. "You won't even know we're there."

Indeed, I never saw them among the few people who came to the short graveside service. Marguerite and Jules had come back from vacation and attended, along with Colette and Jeanne. We were all dressed in black—except for Monique, who stood out from among the others in her rich mauve dress. Instead of being offended, I found that she was the one bright spot in the whole day.

My parents also came to the cemetery, though I hadn't told them when the funeral was to be held. We just stared at each other from across the gaping grave, not knowing what to say. I was close enough to see that they had tears on their cheeks and their eyes were swollen and red. I didn't cry, though, until they lowered the tiny coffin into the dark hole. Then I began to sob, helplessly and horribly. I had lost one more part of myself, and I knew that nothing could ever fill the resulting void in my soul.

A few days later, several lawyers came to see me about testifying at Jacques' trial. I also received my near-perfect scores on my school exams. But that victory seemed hollow now.

A week after Nette's funeral, I went back to work. Marguerite and Jules had canceled the rest of their vacation and were home to stay. Françoise and Colette had gone home, so I was needed again at the cafe. I found relief in work, until closing time, when I went into the kitchen to get Nette ready to take home. A terrible grief washed over me as I realized that she wasn't there, that she wasn't ever going to be there again. Blinking back the tears, I hurried out the door before

Marguerite understood the mistake that had caused me fresh pain. I cried all night, hugging Nette's stuffed bear, and slept in late the next morning. I was getting ready to go down to the cafe when the doorbell rang. It was Monique, but she was not alone. Two young men in white shirts and dark pants were in the hall with her.

"I know you said you didn't want to listen to my friends," she said. "But when I told them about you, they wanted to come and see you. Please, even if you don't want to listen to them, at least let them come in and leave a blessing in your house."

"Oh, Monique," I sighed. "I accepted what you said about there maybe being a heaven, and I'm grateful for the hope it gave me. But I'm not ready to talk about all this. I'm getting back on my feet; isn't that what you wanted?"

"Yes, but I didn't want you to bury your feelings. You're so angry inside. I just want you to understand our Father's plan and learn to be happy again."

Sorrow and pain filled my heart at that. "I don't know if I will ever be happy again," I said. "Or even if I want to be."

"There's one more thing that I have to tell you, Ariana," Monique said, looking at me beseechingly. "I told you Antoine and I had been meeting. What I didn't tell you is that he had also been taking the discussions, the lessons the missionaries have, and that he wanted to be baptized. But he wanted you to hear the lessons first. You were supposed to come with him the day he didn't show up. Think back . . . didn't he mention meeting with me that day?"

I nodded and closed my eyes to stop my tears. "He did, Monique. But this makes no difference now. Please go. I have to go to work."

One of the young men in the poorly lit hallway stepped closer, his features suddenly revealed by the light from my doorway. "Please," he said. "Give us a chance."

I gaped at him. This was the same tall, red-haired missionary who had stopped me by the Seine River two years ago, after Antoine's funeral.

"You!" I exclaimed.

He nodded. "You didn't forget, then," he said. "I wasn't sure if it was you when Monique told us about you—until now. Still, I didn't want to take the chance of missing you. You see, I've always been sure we would meet again. I was supposed to go home two months ago, but I asked for an extension and a transfer back into this area. I kept seeing how your eyes looked that day, and I've wanted the chance to see you again—to teach you."

His voice took me back to the day when I had crumpled up the pamphlet in his face and thrown it to the ground. And how he had not been angry, but kind and loving.

"Did you pray for me?" I asked, a trifle unsteadily.

He nodded vigorously and his voice also shook. "Every single day. I never forgot your face or the look in your eyes. It was as though it had been burned into my memory. I wanted to help you that day we first met, but I couldn't. Please, let me have a chance now." His clear blue eyes bore into mine, imploring.

I started to shake my head, wishing he would go away so I wouldn't have to think about my dead brother or little Nette, just two weeks dead. I pulled my coat tighter around me; the weather had turned exceptionally cold for September, and I would need the coat later on that night. Besides, it seemed I was always so very cold now that Nette wasn't there to warm me with her sunny smiles and affectionate hugs. I thrust my hands deep into the large pockets.

I felt the paper there and brought it out before remembering what it was. There in my hands was the homemade pamphlet the young woman missionary had given me the day after Jacques had left us all those months ago—the day I had told little Nette how she and I were going to be noble queens who ruled themselves and weren't afraid to love and be kind, even though it sometimes hurt so much.

I had to blink twice before my eyes cleared enough to see the picture on the pamphlet. It was of a mother and a baby cuddling, and over it were the words: "You can have your baby with you forever. It's true! Our Heavenly Father has a plan for families."

The pamphlet and the memory of that day decided me. How could I refuse, when I had told Nette how we must be kind despite the pain in our hearts? This missionary wanted, even needed to teach me, and just maybe I needed to hear what he had to say. "Okay," I said finally, looking into the red-haired missionary's pleading eyes. "But not right now. I have to go to work."

"Tomorrow morning, then?"

I shook my head. "I've got an appointment with the Anti-drug Coalition."

"What about the day after—on Saturday? Would ten o'clock be all right?"

I nodded. "But I've got to be to work at noon, so be on time."

I left them without a backward glance, using the stairs instead of waiting for the elevator, hugging my aching memories of Nette to me as tightly as possible so the tears wouldn't come. They had already seen enough of my pain.

All that day, I couldn't keep my mind off the red-haired missionary. I had to admit I was curious. What was it about this church that had made Antoine want to join?

CHAPTER TEN

The next morning Marie, one of the women from the Coalition who had come to my apartment the week before, appeared with three men in tow. She introduced me to the men and they went to work quickly, setting up their lights and cameras. They moved my TV into the kitchen to make room, but brought a large picture of Nette from there to place beside me on the couch.

"Now, here's what's going to happen," Marie said. "You tell your story, and occasionally we might stop you to ask a question or ask you to retell a part of the story. Later, they'll splice everything together to make the commercial. Philippe here," she pointed to a short man with long hair, "will also take photos of you while we videotape—for the posters and billboards. Just try to tell your story the way you did the other day."

I sat on the couch and tried to do as she asked, but couldn't. I kept looking at the cameras and feeling awkward with the strange men watching me. After more than an hour of trying, Marie called it quits.

"Let's take a break, boys." They all stretched and stopped staring into their cameras for a moment. Marie came to sit with me on the couch. "Look," she said to me kindly, "I know this is all kind of awkward, but it really will help others."

"I'm sorry," I said, motioning to the cameras and lights. "I can't seem to do it with all this stuff here." As I spoke, I spied Nette's bear where it had fallen beside the couch during the setting up. I picked it up and held its fluffy white body close to me.

"Was that Nette's?" Marie asked.

I nodded. "I bought it for her when my husband left me, when I was still so full of hope for her," I said. "She didn't pay much attention to it until a couple of months ago, when it became her favorite toy." At that I had to bite my lip to stop it from quivering. "But now she'll never hug or play with it again."

"How did you meet Nette's father?" Marie asked suddenly.

In response to her questions, I slowly told my whole story again in more detail than I had the other night. I told her of our separation, my schooling, and everything leading up to Nette's death. I don't know when I started crying, but suddenly there were tears making their way slowly down my cheeks.

"It's just not fair!" I exclaimed when I'd finished. "My baby never had a chance to even take her first step! Jacques killed her, that's true; but it never would have happened if it hadn't been for the drugs. People have got to realize the ruin that drugs make of lives—and not just our own, but the innocent ones like Nette's!" I hugged the bear tightly and looked down at Nette's picture. "Now my heart aches, my arms are empty, and Nette is gone. It has to stop somewhere—it has to stop *now!*" I looked up at her, my eyes pleading. "Please tell the people."

Marie smiled at me. "I think you just have, Ariana."

"What?"

She motioned to the men, who, unbeknownst to me, were back at their cameras. I saw tears on two of their faces. "It's an old trick, Ariana," Marie said gently. "Pretending to stop filming but not turning off the cameras. I think we'll have enough now to make our commercial. Could we borrow some of Nette's photographs?"

At first I was upset at what Marie had done, but relief came quickly after. Philippe took a few more photographs as the others packed away their equipment and put my apartment back the way it had been. Soon they were ready to leave.

"Thank you so much, Ariana." Marie hugged me as she left. In her hands she held several photographs of Nette. "You're a strong woman. I'll be in touch."

After they left, I cried until I thought my head would explode from the pressure. "Oh, Nette," I moaned over and over in despair, rocking myself to and fro on the floor. "How can I go on without you?"

But I knew that I would.

Abruptly the tide was over, and I went around the apartment and gathered up all pictures, clothes, or any remnants of my baby. I left only the bear and a large picture of Nette in my bedroom, storing the rest in the closet where Monique had already put most of her toys. Someday, I would be able to look at her things without anguish; but I knew that for now, I had to put them away where I would not be assaulted by the memories and the grief at every turn.

I noticed the calendar on the wall. It was September 10th, the same day my brother Antoine had died two years earlier. I was nineteen years and six months old, and I felt that my life was over.

Saturday morning, the missionaries rang the bell ten minutes before I expected them. I opened the door to see their smiling faces. Monique was with them. "We're on time," she said cheerfully.

"No, you're early. But come on in and have a seat anyway." I motioned to the couch with a sweep of my hand.

The missionaries sat on the couch, and Monique and I used the kitchen chairs which I had moved into the living room. The red-haired missionary waited until we were all settled before beginning.

"Well, now, let's properly introduce ourselves. I'm Elder Kenneth Tarr, and this is my companion, Elder Robert Cocteau. We're missionaries from the . . ." The missionary now spoke fluent French but still had a slight American accent. I listened intently, enjoying the sound. Soon he was explaining about prayer and asking Monique to offer one.

I found her prayer curious, yet intriguing—far different from the memorized ones my mother had taught me as a child. Monique talked to God as if he were a real person, someone who actually cared about us individually. And somehow I felt that he really was listening to her.

Afterwards, Elder Tarr began talking about God and Jesus, and the method God always used to communicate to his people—through prophets. "Ariana, this is what he has done in our day,"

Elder Tarr said in a soft voice. "In 1820, there was a young boy named Joseph Smith . . ."

The missionaries took turns explaining about Joseph Smith and the Book of Mormon. They often bore their testimonies, looking sincerely into my eyes as they spoke. Monique also told how she had been converted to the gospel shortly after her parents' deaths. I knew they all believed what they were saying, and I felt strange and wonderful at their words.

"Do you think it is important to know if this book is true?" Elder Cocteau asked me, showing me the book that he claimed Joseph Smith had translated. I nodded and he continued, "It really is important, because if you know it is true, then you will know Joseph Smith is a true prophet of God, and that this is the one true church upon the face of the earth." He turned to a page near the back of the book and showed it to me. It was a promise stating that I could know the truth of this and all things if I but asked. "This is yours now, Ariana," he added, handing me the book.

I took it and promised to read several sections that were marked. We also set up another appointment for the following Monday. I waited for them to leave, but Elder Tarr looked at me. "Would you offer a closing prayer for us?" he asked.

"I don't know how," I said, remembering the easy, eloquent prayer Monique had offered.

"Well, you simply say, 'Heavenly Father,' and then thank him and/or ask him for what you need. Then close in the name of Jesus Christ."

"Okay," I said softly, surprising even myself. I wasn't completely sure I even believed in God. We knelt on the carpet around the coffee table, and I glanced about nervously until the others bowed their heads and closed their eyes. Finally, I closed my own.

"Heavenly Father," I began hesitantly. "Thank you for my friends. Please help me to know if you exist and if you love me." His certain love was something they had stressed during the discussion, but I couldn't understand how he could love me and still let Nette and Antoine die. "And please," my voice broke, "if there is a heaven, please take care of my baby. In the name of Jesus Christ, amen."

We were all crying when we stood up, but I didn't know exactly why. For the first time since Nette's death, I felt strangely comforted. After that we stood around looking awkwardly at each other for a while, then finally the elders left. Monique stayed. I still had over an hour before work, so I asked her if she wanted some coffee.

She shook her head. "No, I don't drink coffee, Ariana. It's got caffeine in it, you know, and that stuff's a drug. It's even addicting."

I thought about what she was saying. "I guess you're right. I never thought about it that way, probably because it doesn't do damage like other drugs."

"Yes, it does," she insisted.

I didn't argue because she was a nurse and would know better. I poured my cup of coffee down the drain and had juice instead.

"Tea is bad, too," Monique said suddenly. "Not the herbal kind, though."

I raised my eyebrows. "Anything else?"

"Just drugs and alcohol and stuff like that. Anything that harms the body."

Light suddenly dawned. "Does this have something to do with your church?"

"Well, yes, but not just. You see, the Prophet Joseph Smith received a revelation counseling the early members not to use such things, years before our doctors began finding out they were bad for our bodies. That was one of the reasons I looked into the Church in the first place. It was incredible to me that an uneducated man could be so right."

"Anyone who counsels against drugs can't be too bad," I said. I found I liked the idea of such a standard for a church. "I wish I had had an influence like that in my life. Maybe then—" I broke off abruptly.

"Ariana, would you like to go to church with me tomorrow?" Monique asked, covering my sudden silence. "Our ward meets in the morning."

I thought of the church services my parents had taken me to at Christmas or for christenings. I had never felt comfortable there. Still, I had nothing else to do, and Monique was good company. And I had to admit that I was very curious. "Okay," I agreed. "Though I don't have anything appropriate to wear. My few good dresses that fit are pretty worn. Some of my dresses from before my marriage are still in great condition, but I'm bigger in some spots now. Not that you can tell, I was such a twig back then." *Before I had Nette,* I added silently, feeling the emptiness in my arms again.

"Let me see them," Monique said suddenly. "You're still thin; they can't be all that difficult to fix." I took her to my room and pulled two dresses from the closet. They were expensive, well-cut dresses that my mother had bought at her favorite shop. Monique turned them inside out immediately. "Why, this can be let out a little, and I think I could add some material to the other. Try it on for me, and let's see what's what." I tried each on in turn. The waist was fine on both, but the hip and bust were definitely too tight.

I found some thread and Monique went deftly to work, pulling out the stitches and placing tiny, even ones of her own. "This one I can do by hand, but the other I'll take with me. I have a machine at home." Her fingers flew in and out so quickly that they were merely a blur.

"So where did you learn this?" I asked enviously. "Is it one more thing your grandmother taught you?" My own grandmother had died before I was born, during the long years my parents had tried to have a child.

"Oh, no," Monique said quickly. "My grandmother hated sewing. But after she and I joined the Church, the sisters in the ward taught me. We get together once a month, or more often if necessary, to teach each other different homemaking skills. You would hardly believe the many different talents they have to share." She laughed. "Why, even I have to give a lesson on home remedies next week."

I laughed with her, but wistfully. "I wouldn't have anything to offer," I said.

"Oh, Ariana!" Monique stopped her sewing abruptly. "That's not true! In fact, what you have to offer I think would be a lot more important than what I could ever teach!"

I stared at her in disbelief. *What could I possibly know that Monique didn't?*

My thoughts must have been obvious, for Monique continued softly, "Well, if you don't know, maybe it's best to let you find out for yourself." She put her sturdy hand on my shoulder. "But trust me on this, okay? You have so much to share inside of you. Maybe you're just not ready." She turned back to her sewing while I got ready for work, still puzzling over her words.

That night after closing the cafe, I began to read the book the elders had given me. They had assigned me 3 Nephi chapter 11, but I didn't stop there. I read until chapter 17, where Jesus blessed and wept over the little children. Suddenly, I felt his love around me as tangible as anything I had ever touched. It was amazing to me that though I had always believed I was alone, I never really had been.

I thought of Nette and cried, but this time there was hope mingled with my tears. I knew she was with Jesus and Antoine. I didn't quite understand it all, yet I wanted to. I read far into the night, looking up anything to do with children or resurrection. It wasn't hard; I slipped easily back into my schooling mode. Hours later when I finished reading, I knew for certain that I would see Nette and Antoine again. This knowledge, after the dismal feelings of finality before, made my heart sing. I still hurt terribly and desperately inside, but at least I could see a tunnel and a light at the end. The light was my Savior, Jesus Christ, and I knew that he loved me and understood what I was feeling.

The next morning Monique arrived early, but I was awake and ready in the dress she had let out the day before. I hadn't slept much that night, but I didn't feel the lack; I was alive with questions. "I need more to read about the Church," I told her when she couldn't answer my questions fast enough.

"Okay, okay," she said laughingly. "After church we'll stop off at my apartment and get all the books I have. I have quite a few of them, some I haven't even read. I never was much of a reader."

The church building was quite unlike anything I ever expected. It was large and spacious without being pretentious. There were rows of comfortable benches where whole families were filing in to sit together. On their faces were smiles and loving glances. We were greeted at the door by a friendly man Monique introduced as the bishop. And there was a score of young people who gathered around us excitedly, talking and laughing. Then several sets of missionaries arrived, among them Elders Tarr and Cocteau.

"Hey, Elder, I hear you're finally going home!" someone said to

Elder Tarr. "Or are you going to try and extend again?"

He laughed and shook his head. "No, I think I've done the work I was supposed to do." He looked directly at me as he talked. "Haven't I, Ariana?"

I think I had always known the Church was true, ever since I saw Elder Tarr's kind face on the day of Antoine's funeral. I didn't know how he knew I had accepted the Church, but I did know that he was the only missionary who could have broken through my shell of hurt and anger to make me listen. And it had only taken that once.

"Yes, I want to be baptized," I said softly. "Why didn't you ask me yesterday?"

"Because you weren't ready yet," he replied with a smile. "But how about next Sunday, is that soon enough for you? I go home the Wednesday after."

"I have to wait that long?" I asked. The group of young people around me burst into laughter at my words. I hadn't realized until I spoke that they had all been holding their breaths, waiting for my reply.

"Well, we need to give you the rest of the discussions," Elder Tarr replied. "Just to make sure you understand the covenants you will be making." We confirmed the appointment we had already made for Monday, and made two more for later in the week. They would teach me two discussions the first two days and the final one on Friday.

"And you might want to start thinking about people you want to invite to your baptism," Elder Tarr added. "It's a very good way to share the gospel with someone."

I immediately thought of my parents, but the gulf between us was so great that I didn't know how to go about breaching it. I knew that inside, I partly blamed them for my life since Antoine died, and especially for Nette's death. *Why hadn't they wanted me?* I shut out the feelings quickly because I wasn't ready to deal with them. Someday, perhaps, when my wounds weren't so fresh.

The week went by quickly in a flurry of reading and learning. On Wednesday, the missionaries taught me the fourth and fifth discussions. They showed me the film, "Families Can Be Together Forever." I found myself crying when the boy's mother died; I knew so well what he was feeling. "Are you all right, Ariana?" Elder Tarr asked me, concern apparent in his eyes.

I nodded. "It's just that I wish I had listened to you two years ago. I can't help but think what a lot of pain I could have spared myself . . . and my baby."

The elder's sadness glistened in his eyes, but we both knew nothing could change the past. "Sometimes we don't always understand why things happen, Ariana, but we must trust in the Lord. He knows what he's doing. And whether we appreciate the trials or not, we always learn and grow from them."

"Well, I'd like to stay this size for a while, if you don't mind," I said, trying to make my voice light.

My tone didn't fool Elder Tarr. He gazed at me sincerely as he spoke. "I think you will, Ariana. The Lord knows you better than anyone, and he knows when the growing needs to ease up. But never forget that the Father loves those he tests. If he didn't care, he wouldn't want us to progress and become more like him. That's what the trials do for us, you know. They make us more like him. And I believe with my whole heart that he suffers right along with us."

I nodded. We had always wanted to be queens, Nette and I. We just hadn't realized exactly what kind. And I knew that to be like our Heavenly King would be even more difficult than I had thought—but also much more rewarding in the end.

That Sunday, three and a half weeks after Nette's death, I was baptized. It was a beautiful, cloudless day in late September. Marguerite, Jules, and my next-door neighbor, Jeanne, attended. Marguerite was mostly disapproving, feeling as though I was being taken advantage of because of Nette's death. But even she felt the Spirit at the baptismal meeting and shed a few tears. Jeanne came gratefully, happy to know I didn't blame her for what Jacques had done. We hadn't talked much since that terrible day, but slowly our relationship was returning to normal.

I emerged from the warm water feeling new and reborn. As I received the Holy Ghost, I knew there would still be many trials ahead in my life, but now I would never feel alone again. Not only would my Savior be near, but I would also have the constant companionship of the Holy Ghost.

Life changed drastically after my baptism. When I wasn't at work,

I was involved in Church service. Almost immediately, I was put into the Young Women organization, where I learned by teaching. I avidly read every Church book I could get my hands on, and spent hours researching my lessons.

Church was much like an extended family, and I loved being there. People were friendly and caring. There were many young adults my age; but while I enjoyed being with them, and maybe even resembled them on the outside, I realized that my experiences distanced me from them. Not in a bad way, but in a way that actually made my observations and comments help them understand life and the gospel. Monique was right; I did have something important to offer them. In turn, the older sisters helped me come to terms with my loss, as well as the anger and guilt that still burned in my soul. Slowly, as the weeks and months went by, the pain I felt at Nette's passing dimmed in the light and love of the gospel.

Of course, I still found time in my busy schedule to volunteer once a week at the Anti-drug Coalition and make a few personal appearances. The new media campaign was a huge success, and the Coalition received not only many new calls for help but also much additional funding. It also meant that my face was plastered from one end of France to the other, and often I felt embarrassed when people would recognize me in the street. I cut my hair very short again to reduce such recognition, and to some extent it worked.

My divorce from Jacques went through in the middle of November, and shortly after he went to prison. I learned about it when the lawyer prosecuting the case came to see me at work. "He's pleaded guilty so you won't need to testify against him," he said. "It's just as well, because our main witness, Paulette, has disappeared somewhere. She wasn't too reliable anyway because of her drug habit."

I drank in the information slowly. "I haven't seen her since that night," I said. "I haven't wanted to." I felt guilty as I said it, but I was telling the truth. "How long will Jacques go to prison for?"

"Well, the judge will decide next week, but since he was under the influence of drugs at the time, he probably won't get more than seven years. That means with time off for good behavior, he'll probably serve around five."

It didn't seem like much of a punishment for all the years he had taken away from Nette, but I didn't get upset. I told myself that ultimate punishment would come from the Lord. Meanwhile, I couldn't help but hope that Jacques would be miserable in prison.

"So where do you go from here?" the man asked me curiously. He really seemed to want to know. Maybe it was because he had three little ones of his own and needed to know how I could cope with my loss.

"Well, I'm starting school in accounting in January," I said. "From there, I'll take one day at a time. I know I'll see my daughter again someday." I began to explain some of my beliefs, and even gave him a pamphlet with the missionaries' number on it.

"Thanks," he said as he left. "Maybe I'll check it out."

The year passed quickly for me. I kept busy learning, teaching, and just plain surviving. For the most part I did well, except when it rained at night. Then I was alone, so very alone. Often I would relive Nette's death—and Antoine's, as well. During those nights, only my growing testimony of the Lord kept me sane. Crazily, I found that at those times I even missed Jacques.

"You'll find someone else," Monique assured me. Indeed, she kept trying to introduce me to every eligible bachelor in the Church. Those I did date either weren't my type, or they couldn't see beyond my past. I told myself it didn't matter. But deep inside, where I didn't let anyone see, I hoped I would find someone special. At times I despaired that it would ever happen. I felt so lonely and unfulfilled.

Until I met Jean-Marc, and my life once more changed forever.

CHAPTER ELEVEN

It was in January, three months before I turned twenty-one, over a year since my baptism, that Elder Jean-Marc Perrault, from Bordeaux in the southwest of France, was transferred into my area. From the moment I set eyes on him, I knew that somehow he was different than any of the other missionaries who had come before.

He wasn't much taller than me, and I had never been very tall, but he was large in presence. He was my age, nearly two years older than most of the other missionaries, and was incredibly handsome, with black hair and wonderful green-brown eyes. He had an engaging grin, yet a serious way about him that appealed to me.

"I know you," he said to me the first day he saw me. It was Sunday, and Monique and I had just arrived at the chapel for an early morning meeting called by the missionaries in our ward. We had been introduced to the new missionary, and since then he had been staring at me curiously. "You've cut your hair, though, and you're much prettier in—" He broke off abruptly, as if suddenly remembering he was a missionary, albeit one only out two months and still not quite used to the mantle he'd been given.

We all laughed at his expression. "Yes, that's me on the TV commercials," I admitted.

"Don't worry about it, Elder Perrault," said his companion, Elder Jones from America. "We all forget ourselves the first time we meet Ariana." We laughed some more, but I could see that Elder Perrault wanted to ask me if what the commercials said was true; everyone always asked me that, even though the commercial came right out and said it was a true story before I even began talking. Usually I didn't like to dwell on my loss, but somehow I felt it important that this particular missionary understand the truth about me right from the first.

"It's all true," I said quietly to him as the others dispersed.

His eyes locked onto mine. "Somehow I knew you wouldn't lie about such a thing. I'm so sorry."

I smiled wistfully. "I've gone on now, and I know I'll see her and raise her someday. I'm stronger for it."

"Yes, I guess you are." The look he gave me was admiring, without pity. "Anyway, I'm pleased to meet you after all this time. To tell the whole truth, I'd hoped to meet you one day."

"It's nice to meet you, too, Elder," I returned, though I was thinking it was a little strange that he should want to meet me because of my commercials. Usually men seemed turned off when they heard about my past. But then Elder Perrault was a missionary, and he certainly didn't mean he had wanted to meet me in the romantic sense . . . or did he?

I was saved from having to think about it further when Elder Jones motioned for us to sit so that he could begin the meeting. After a song and a prayer, he got right to the point. "We need volunteers to help with the missionary work," Elder Jones said. "Those who want to help will be divided into member missionary teams to work with the different missionaries in your area. They will visit you each week and help you understand how to do missionary work with your friends and relatives and set specific goals to reach. Our mission president feels that by working through our members, we will not only find and baptize more people, but have them stay active because of your love and support for them. We need every one of you. Now who wants to volunteer?"

I raised my hand immediately. Ever since a year ago, when I had talked to the lawyer who was prosecuting Jacques' case, I had wanted to learn how to share the gospel. I always felt so strange and unsure of myself when talking about it with others. Even when prompted, I didn't know what to say.

We divided into teams. Monique and I were put together with

another girl, Aimee, and a young man named Claude. We were assigned to Elders Jones and Perrault, the missionaries in our area.

"Well," began Elder Perrault, looking at the other teams who each had at least twice as many members, "we're outnumbered. But we all know that quality is better than quantity." We laughed.

"What we want you to do is to make a list of ten friends or family by the time we visit you this week," Elder Jones said. "People you love or those you feel might be open to hearing about the gospel."

"And you don't have to worry that we're going to beat down their doors," joked Elder Perrault, as if reading my thoughts. "We just want you to have the names on paper so we can discuss them and what steps you can take to make their introduction to the Church a positive one."

"Will you do that?" Elder Jones asked each of us in turn. We all committed ourselves.

I struggled with my list that week, taking their challenge seriously and prayerfully. Though I had many friends in the Church, I hadn't reached out to any nonmembers since Nette's death. Marguerite and Jules were already at the top of my list, but I was plagued with doubts about who to put next. To make things worse, it rained all week because of a sudden warming in the weather. I was reminded forcefully of Nette and Antoine, and spent much of the week crying alone in the night. *It really doesn't rain much in Paris,* I thought ironically. *Only when I have trouble.*

Luckily, I had school and work to keep me busy. I was in my second year of accounting and enjoying it thoroughly. Soon I would be looking for a job in my field, and leaving the cafe behind forever. That was one of the reasons why Marguerite and Jules were on my list. I owed them so much, and yet couldn't find a way to share with them the most precious gift I could—the gospel.

The rest of my list grew slowly: Jeanne and her husband; Dauphine, the girl who worked the cafe in the mornings; a certain regular at the cafe; and one girl at school. This brought me up to seven people. And there it stayed. I knew deep down who at least two of the remaining three people should be, but I couldn't write their names. Not yet.

"Well, let's see that list," Elder Perrault said to me on Friday afternoon, when he and his companion appeared at the appointed time at the cafe where I was taking a break.

I gave it to him reluctantly. "I've only got the seven—so far," I confessed. "But I want to have more."

He smiled at me and ran a hand through his thick, black hair as if to push it back, forgetting that it was already cut very short and no longer needed such attention. "We'll work on it, Ariana," he said. "That's what we're here for." The way he said my name seemed caressing, but he was unaware of it—or of how my heart beat so quickly when he was near. I was surprised to find myself reacting to him that way. It was the first time it had happened since Jacques. Not one of the men Monique had introduced me to had made me feel anything similar.

Instead of pressuring me about the rest of the list, Elder Perrault talked with me about Marguerite and Jules and what I could do to help them. "You love them, don't you?" he asked me after we had gone over the steps of missionary work.

"More than anyone alive, besides Monique," I said.

"Then you have already finished many of the steps. Now you need to prayerfully decide how to approach them. Remember, the only thing they can say is no. It shouldn't change your relationship."

"So should I ask them to meet with you?"

Elder Jones shook his head. "Maybe try something else first. How about asking them to church? They believe in God, don't they? Church is a good way for them to feel the Spirit without being threatened."

"All right, I'll do it," I said determinedly. It did seem a lot easier to ask Marguerite and Jules to church than to ask them to listen to the discussions. After the elders left, I began fasting with a goal to ask them to go to church with me on Sunday. But the rain continued and I felt despondent. No matter how I tried, I couldn't seem to find an opportunity to ask them. When Saturday evening rolled slowly to a close, I knew that it was now or never.

"Uh, Marguerite," I began hesitantly as we finished putting away the food. I could hear Jules in the office, putting the day's proceeds into the safe. "You know, you and Jules have been like family to me these past two and a half years . . ." My voice trailed off. I didn't know how to continue.

"As you have been to us, Ariana."

I plunged on. "Well, after Nette's death, I found my church, and I know you thought I was jumping into things. But I've been very happy there, haven't I?"

Marguerite nodded. "Yes, I think I was wrong. It's been very good for you."

"Well, I wanted to know if you and Jules would come to church with me tomorrow. I think you might enjoy it there. And it would be nice to spend some time together outside of work. What do you think?" I stopped talking and began to hold my breath. I was so afraid she would say no.

"That sounds nice," Marguerite said, as if it were the most natural question in the world. "I think I'd enjoy going. Jules and I haven't been inside a church since we buried our Michelle. Maybe it's time we go back. I'll tell Jules about it, but I'm sure he'll come."

I wanted to tell them what to expect, to prepare them for the difference from their own church, but something stilled my tongue. Maybe the true church was best experienced.

The next morning the January sun shone weakly but insistently over Paris, and my depression had completely lifted. Jules, Marguerite, and I all went to church in Jules' car. There they were greeted with the same love and enthusiasm I had experienced more than a year before. I saw the amazement on their faces at the simple beauty of the chapel and the services. Afterward, I proudly introduced them to the elders.

"I do believe you can do anything you set your mind to, Ariana," Elder Perrault said to me privately. I thought again that his deep voice was tender, and I blushed like a child. Seeing my discomfort, he grinned. But he didn't understand that I was reacting to him and not his compliments.

Things went quickly after that, with the missionaries giving Marguerite and Jules the first discussion the very next day. The elders also began to come daily to the cafe for lunch, where Marguerite clucked over them like a mother hen and Jules regaled them with stories of his youth. Two weeks later, the elders and I taught the

Geoffrins the fourth discussion. As they heard and understood how families can be eternal, I knew for certain that they had finally accepted the gospel.

"You mean we can be sealed to Michelle?" Marguerite asked. "We will see her again and be a family?"

I nodded. "It's part of the plan our Father has for us. We're all going back to live with him someday, if we are worthy, to become more and more like him, and to inherit his kingdom."

Her gaze was intent. "Then everything you used to tell little Nette about being a queen someday was real," she said with sudden insight. "She is going to be a queen someday, isn't she?"

Tears came to my eyes and I couldn't speak. But Elder Perrault said softly, "Yes, just like her mother." My eyes flew to his in surprise. How could he know how I struggled to act as a queen would, to be worthy of raising my baby one day?

"Based on our worthiness, we will all be like our Heavenly King," Elder Jones added. "But first we have to live our lives in . . ." He continued on, leading the conversation away from the doctrine that was generally hard for investigators to understand. But I knew instinctively that he was wrong in this case; we all needed to know about Nette and how my dreams for her would come true, even though she was dead.

A week later, Marguerite and Jules were baptized, and attending the special meeting were the next five people on my list. The missionary spirit burned in my soul, and suddenly it was easy to share the gospel. I felt the Lord really did bless those who opened their mouths despite their fears and insecurities.

Over the next month, our member missionary team worked hard to bring the gospel to those on our lists. We began baptizing new members almost every week, to the surprise of the other teams who had not yet gotten so involved. In the first week of March, after working almost daily with Elder Perrault and his companion, we baptized the rest of the seven people on my list, along with some of their friends and family.

"You've done better than you expected, haven't you?" Elder Perrault asked me that Sunday.

I smiled. "Yes. I was scared at first, but now it seems to come easily."

"You'll make a good missionary," he said with a special light in his eyes. His companion beside him nodded in agreement.

I stared at him in wonder. "Me?" In the last few months I had often longed to go, but because of my past, I didn't think they would let me. Even so, my desire to serve a mission had increased as my twenty-first birthday grew closer. Now it was little more than a week away.

"Why not, Ari?" Elder Perrault asked.

His sudden use of my old nickname froze me in my place. For a long moment I couldn't breathe as I stood and stared at him. Then finally, my throat loosened up and I could speak. "Ariana," I whispered hoarsely. "Not Ari. Still not Ari." And despite my efforts to the contrary, I began to cry. I turned and fled out the door, with the elders looking anxiously after me.

Rain drizzled slowly but incessantly the next day when the elders came to see me at the cafe. It was my day off, but we had planned to meet because of the missionary team. As usual, Marguerite fussed over them and introduced them to everyone who came into the building. But at last I was left alone with the elders.

"How are you?" Elder Perrault asked with concern. He looked as if he had not slept well the night before, and since he refused any food, I knew he was fasting.

"I'm okay," I said. "I'm sorry about yesterday. There are just some things I haven't told anyone about . . . about my family."

The elders and I were seated at a table in the corner of the nearly deserted cafe. Elder Jones pulled out his notebook and retrieved my sheet of names. The last three spots were still blank.

"What about your family?" Elder Perrault asked me, indicating the list in his companion's hands. "Why aren't they on this sheet?"

I sighed and closed my eyes for a minute. The rain fell softly against the window in a continual assault, and I wanted to scream at it to stop. "I hate the rain," I said suddenly. "Why does it have to rain so much?"

Elder Perrault stared at me, his expression sincere, his lips moving slightly as if in prayer. He was going to say something, but his companion beat him to it. "It doesn't rain all that much here," Elder

Jones said. "You ought to see how much it rains in Washington, where I'm from."

I didn't care in the slightest how much it rained in Washington, so I sat there silently.

Elder Perrault looked hard at his companion, then turned to me. "It has been wetter than in past years, so I've been told. I think—"

"I guess I just notice it more than others," I interrupted bitterly.

Elder Perrault didn't even blink at my retort, but sat watching me. His handsome face was calm, his eyes caring. When he spoke, his voice was soft yet compelling. "Tell me, what happened to make you hate the rain?"

I took a deep breath. I found that I wanted to tell him. I wanted to bury myself in his arms and tell him everything. Of course, I couldn't do the latter, but I could at least explain. "I had a brother once—Antoine," I began suddenly, before I could change my mind. "We're twins. My parents tried for many years to have a baby, and finally they did. Only they had two instead of just one. Antoine was everything I ever could want in a brother. Everyone adored him, my parents included. He had a way with people, yet he never abused his gift. I loved him so much." Tears rolled slowly down my cheeks, and I brushed them away impatiently. "He used to call me Ari. Everyone did. Three years ago, he died on a rainy day like this one. My parents shut down inside themselves, and I felt that Ari was gone forever, buried in the earth with Antoine. I went crazy for awhile, but finally settled down and had Nette. Then she died." I paused and gave them a watery smile, trying desperately to stifle the sobs that threatened to burst from my throat. "It was raining that night, too."

"And you never see your parents?"

"Once, a few months before Nette died, and then again at her funeral." I looked at them seriously. "I know they are supposed to be two of the last three people on my list, but I don't know if I am able to contact them, or if they even want me."

"How could they not want you, Ari?" asked Elder Perrault with tears in his eyes. The eyes suddenly widened when he realized he had called me Ari again. "I'm sorry. You just look like an Ari to me. Over the months I have thought of you as such, but no one ever used the name. I finally decided to see how you liked it. I'm very sorry. I won't do it again if you don't want me to."

I smiled slightly. "It doesn't hurt so much today, now that you know about my brother," I said, surprised to be telling the truth. "And if there ever was anyone to call me that, it should be you." Now I had to choose my words carefully, because he was still a missionary and I wouldn't compromise his calling for anything. "You are very special, like my brother was. You are very similar."

"Then that makes two of us," he replied. "You are also very like you described Antoine." He paused and added softly, "So what do you think he would do in relation to your parents?"

I laughed shortly, but without real mirth. "I knew you would ask that. I've asked myself the same question almost every day for the past year. Maybe it's time for me to talk with them. Maybe I can finally do it."

"You can, Ari. I know you can." Elder Perrault looked so confident that I felt I really could do it.

"Did you mean what you said about me being a missionary?" I asked suddenly. "Would they accept someone who has been married and had a child?" Both missionaries nodded.

"You'll be wonderful!" Elder Perrault smiled at me and I felt myself tingle all over in a way that I, a woman who had been married and given birth, barely recognized. "And I'll write to you every week."

My eyes met his. "Really?"

"I guarantee it." His eyes were full of promise.

The next morning the sun was shining brightly again, making my spirit warm. Eagerly I went to see my bishop at his work without calling. He was a supervisor at the local telephone company and was in his office most of the day.

"I want to go on a mission," I blurted out the second his secretary left the room. "Can I go? Even though I've been married before?" I didn't mention the fact that I'd also had a baby; Bishop Rameau already knew my history.

He was silent for a moment and I held my breath, fearing his answer. "Oh, Ariana," he said finally, "I think that's a wonderful idea. I don't know why I didn't think of it myself. You will be an exceptional missionary." His face was so sincere that for a moment I wanted to cry. "But I think because your divorce took place after your baptism, you will need an interview with a member of the Area Presidency."

"What! Why?" I asked, nervous again at the thought of actually talking alone with a General Authority. They were men to be revered.

Bishop Rameau seemed to read my mind. "They are people, as we are, but with a special calling. There's nothing to be afraid of. As to why you need to see him, it's just Church policy for youth who have been divorced. But I think you will enjoy the encounter."

I didn't agree, but nodded anyway. "So how soon can I do this? I want to go on my mission as soon as possible." I knew that even once the interviews were completed and the papers sent, I would have to wait weeks, maybe months, for my call.

He smiled. "I'll bring the papers to the cafe this evening. It won't take long to fill them out. I'll make an appointment with the stake president for Sunday, and he'll make one with the Area Presidency for whenever one of them is available. I'll tell him how anxious you are."

I wasn't sure that was a good idea, but I thanked him and left.

As promised, Bishop Rameau brought the mission papers by the cafe that evening. By Sunday, two days before my birthday, they were completed and ready to go, and I was interviewed by my bishop and the stake president. I was happy and content that they were both excited and positive about my decision.

But, as I walked out of the room where the stake president had held my interview, I was startled to see an American man in a dark suit. By his very posture, I knew he was a General Authority, though I didn't recognize him personally. Bishop Rameau was at his side and introduced the man by name. I heard only "Elder"; the rest of the name escaped me.

"He came today because I told him how anxious you are to go on your mission," the stake president explained as I shook hands with the tall man. "He is flying to Utah tomorrow to counsel with the brethren and won't be back for several weeks. He wasn't sure he was going to make it today, but he did."

I smiled faintly. I was happy that I wouldn't have to wait weeks for my interview, but mentally unprepared for it today. "Thank you,"

I said mechanically.

The man smiled and motioned to the room we had just left.

"You don't want a translator?" Bishop Rameau asked.

"I think not," the man replied in heavily accented French. "Thank you." He gestured again and I went inside. He followed me and closed the door. I gulped audibly; I was alone with a General Authority.

He began our interview by asking me brief questions about my life and my desire to serve a mission. His French was bad and my English worse, but somehow we communicated. He was well-informed of my past, thanks to Bishop Rameau, who spoke fluent English, and it made things easier for me. Even so, I was in tears as I told him about my baby. To my surprise, he was also crying. I watched as large tears rolled slowly down his long face, and I wondered that he could feel so much for me, someone he didn't even know. It reminded me of how the Savior loved. Truly this was a man of God!

"Ariana," he said after we had talked for over an hour, "I feel that your Father in Heaven loves you very much, and is pleased with the way you are living your life. In his estimation and in mine, you are worthy in every way to serve a mission."

I didn't know what language he was speaking, but I understood him perfectly. With tears streaming down my face and blocking my vision, I said, "Oh, thank you. Thank you so much."

"No," he said, shaking his head, "thank you, Ariana. Thank you."

We were quiet for a comfortable moment. I felt as if I had known this man all my life, and I didn't even know his name.

"Can we pray?" he asked.

I nodded mutely. We knelt down on the rough carpet and he began to pray. He called down the blessings of heaven upon me and pleaded with the Lord in my behalf. I had never felt so much love before. It permeated my whole being until I couldn't hold another drop.

When he was done, I hugged him; I couldn't help myself. I wanted to thank him again, but my voice would not obey. It didn't matter because I knew he understood; we had been communicating with our spirits.

As I left the room, he held up my papers. "I'll take care of these, Ariana. You'll get your calling soon. You're going to be a wonderful missionary!"

I left him, my heart full of love and singing with joy. But as I walked down the street to the metro, it started to rain softly, making me recall my conversation of the previous week with Elder Perrault, and how he had made me feel that it was time for me to see my parents. With this new love inside of me, I suddenly knew I couldn't leave on a mission without clearing things up with them. I had to at least tell them I loved them, regardless of the distance and bad feelings between us.

Darkness was already beginning to fall when I arrived near the expensive apartment building where my parents lived. As I hesitated outside, several people came out of the lower door and held it open for me so that I wouldn't have to use my nonexistent key to open it. I thanked them and smiled, but as soon as they were out of sight I left the building and let the door shut behind me. Then I went to stand before the row of buttons that would ring in the individual apartments above. It wasn't fair for me to simply appear outside my parents' door; I would at least give them the few minutes it would take for me to reach their fourth-floor apartment to prepare themselves for my visit, as I had tried to prepare myself on the way over. I pushed the black buzzer and waited for an answer.

Suddenly I was afraid.

CHAPTER TWEVLE

Who is it?" came my mother's voice through the speaker.

"It's Ariana. May I come up?"

I heard a swift intake of breath and a shocked pause. Then the buzzer at the door sounded as the outside door unlocked. I made my way up to their apartment slowly, using the stairs instead of the elevator to give them more time. I imagined my mother rushing into the sitting room to tell my father I was coming. Would they be planning what to say? Or would they simply look at each other without speaking, their hearts racing as wildly as mine? Or maybe they didn't care. I didn't quite believe that last thought, though it made no difference; whether they accepted me or not, I had to make my peace with them before I could serve the Lord on a mission. It was something I had to do.

The fact that it was raining outside didn't escape me, and a sense of impending doom was constant. But I pressed on regardless. Suddenly I was at the door, and it opened before I rang.

"Come in, Ariana," my mother said softly. Her expression was hopeful, and for the first time I had the inkling that maybe I had judged her wrongly in the last few years.

We went to the sitting room and sat down. It was clean and elegant and looked nearly the same as when Antoine and I had lived there. Memories of happy times when I was a child chased each other through my mind. I also saw my parents as they had been then—young, hopeful, and loving.

I sat on a comfortable chair opposite the sofa where my parents were settling themselves. In the quiet of the room, I studied them. They seemed older than before, and somehow softer. I couldn't help hoping that the last year and a half since Nette's death had changed them as it had changed me.

"I came because I wanted to say that I am sorry for the past few years," I began, looking at the floor, feeling like a small child again. I was certainly grateful that I had rehearsed my speech on the way over. Maybe I would finally be able to tell them everything. "For years I've hated you for blocking me out after Antoine died. Instead of his death bringing us together, it tore us apart. I blamed you both for everything that happened afterwards—my drinking, doing drugs, even getting pregnant. I was just so lonely, and you weren't there." I began to cry silently. The tears fell from my eyes, but I paid them no heed. "Then you came to me after Nette was born, and I hoped deep inside that you wanted to be a family again. But instead you asked for Nette—the one thing I had left in my life. You wanted her, not me." I looked up at them now. "Don't you see that I needed you, that I just wanted your love?"

"We do love you, Ariana!" they said together.

My mother came to kneel next to my chair. The bright light from the lamp nearby lit up her face, and I could see the love in her eyes quite clearly. "We *did* want you in our lives. We were just afraid that we were too late. We feared that how we acted when your brother died pushed you so far away that you'd never be able to forgive us!"

My father also came to kneel by my mother. The telling light showed that he was no longer stiff and withdrawn, but reaching out to me with hope. "We asked to take care of Nette, but we meant for you both to come back here to live with us." He gazed at me earnestly with tears in his eyes. "We wanted to help you, but we didn't know what to do!"

I nodded, looking at each of them in turn. "I think I knew inside that you loved me—or wanted to believe it. But I guess even when Antoine was alive, I knew I was always second-best."

"What?" my parents said again in chorus, seeming genuinely surprised.

"But we've always loved you, Ariana," my mother said. "As much as we ever loved Antoine."

I shook my head. "No. No one was ever like Antoine. He was special. And I didn't mind being second to him."

"But you're special, too!" my mother said. "The way you always knew how to bring a smile to our faces. The way you always stuck up for what you believed in. We loved you every bit as much as we loved Antoine. You have your own special talents, some similar to your brother and some very different."

I felt the truth of her words spread through me, but I wasn't ready to let it go that easily. "But you always treated him differently. You let him do what he wanted, and yet I couldn't go to the corner flea market without company!"

"That is true," my father said. "We did want to protect you from people like . . . like Jacques and Paulette, and Antoine always was a good judge of character. But our wanting you to be with him was for him as well as for you. You were always a steadying influence on him. We hoped that your common sense would rub off on him, even just a little. He could be so impulsive at times, but when he thought he was taking care of you, he was always more responsible."

"I never saw that in him," I said, but as the words came, I remembered that my brother had been impulsive, doing daredevil things that he would never let me do. I remembered how once I had cried out in fear that he would fall off a steep wall to his death, and how he had promised me to never do such a thing again. My brother had been wonderful, full of infectious laughter, caring, and trust-worthy. But he had also been heedless of many hidden consequences, things that had been so clear to me. Maybe I had been as important to him as he had been to me.

If only I had been with him on the morning he died.

"Can you ever forgive us?" my father asked. "For what happened to you after Antoine died, as well as for Nette's death?"

I started at his words. "But that's really what I came to tell you. I don't blame you anymore for any of it. I've learned that we all make our own decisions and have to live with them, and some things, like death, aren't even in our control. What happened wasn't your fault or mine; it was just because we didn't know any better."

"Will you . . . come back home?" my mother asked hesitantly.

I didn't know until she asked that I even wanted to come home, that I longed for my parents to want me with them.

"Do you really want me to?" I asked.

"Yes, we do," my father replied. "We always have. We need you."

I smiled through my tears. "Then I want to come. But I will only be able to stay a month or so, and then I'm going on a mission."

"A mission?"

As I talked, I prayed they would understand. "Well, after Nette's death, I was in a bad way, but I had a good friend who helped me a lot. And through her I found that the true church of God has been restored to the earth! My whole life has changed now—that's part of the reason I came tonight—and I want to go out to tell other people about it."

My mother looked steadily at my father in the lamplight, and then at me. "Any religion that brought you back to us must be good."

"How long will you be gone?" My father was more practical.

"A year and a half." I saw their sadness at that, so I hurried to add, "But I'll write to you every week, and I probably won't even go for six weeks or more. I haven't gotten my call—my assignment—yet. But it's something I have to do."

"You're an adult," my father said, "and you make your own decisions. But we had simply hoped for more time. We have so much to make up for."

"But that's just it, Father," I said earnestly. "We'll have plenty of time. With each other, and with Antoine and Nette. That's what so wonderful about the gospel—knowing there's so much more than what we see. We can be a family forever, even after death!"

My parents appeared skeptical, but they didn't reply or verbally reject what I had said. That alone showed how much they had changed.

The next day, Monday, I moved back home after my morning classes, even though I would lose the last two weeks' rent from my old apartment. It was worth it. It was worth almost anything to have my family back. And Marguerite and Jules weren't upset in the least, only very happy that I had patched things up with my parents.

"I always knew they loved you," Marguerite said. She hugged me and then sent Jules to help move my things.

"So now what?" my mother asked as we settled my few belongings in my old, familiar bedroom. It had been kept virtually the way I had left it years ago. Since it was fully furnished, my other possessions such as Nette's toys and clothing, and my couch and bed—the only furniture really worth keeping—went into my parents' storage shed in the basement of our building.

"Well, I'm going to finish out my school course and work until I get my mission call."

"But you don't need to work anymore," she protested, trying to hide her grimace as she unpacked my worn clothing. "We want to take care of you while you're in school."

I stood up and took her hands in mine, looking earnestly into her eyes. "I know, Mother, and I'm so grateful. But I'm trying to earn as much as I can to pay for my mission, so my church doesn't have to do it."

"You have to pay money to go?"

"Only my expenses—food, clothing, a place to stay."

"Oh." My mother's voice was thoughtful.

I forgot about our conversation until later that night, when my father knocked softly on the door. I had just settled into bed, and called for him to come in.

"Your mother tells me that you have to pay for this mission of yours," he said bluntly. "I'd like to help you out." He held up his hand before I could speak. "We've got more than enough money to do so. And it would make us feel better, knowing that we are helping our little girl."

His words reminded me of how much I'd wanted to give to Nette, and how time had taken away that chance. "Thank you, Father," I said, knowing what it meant to him for me to accept. It meant a great deal to me, too. I could almost feel the weight of my monetary worries vanishing as if they had never existed. "I would appreciate it greatly."

"I also want you to come to work for me at the bank," he said, reaching out to hold my hand. I was almost overwhelmed at the love I felt in his grasp. "You'd earn a lot more money, and when you come back you'd have a good job waiting. You'd be good, too, from what you tell us of your grades, and you'd learn a lot."

A job at the bank! "Oh, Father, I would love to!" I blurted out without thinking. Then I remembered the cafe. "But I'd have to talk to Marguerite first."

"Of course." He kissed my cheeks and left.

I lay in bed thinking of the new life opening up before me. My parents back, a good job. If only . . . Thoughts of Nette overcame me, and I held her bear to my chest tightly. But I didn't cry. Suddenly I was thinking of Elder Perrault, and how my heart fluttered every time I saw him. Quitting work at the cafe would mean that I wouldn't see him every day, only on Sundays. But maybe that would be for the best, in view of how I felt about him and the fact that he was a missionary.

I fell asleep thinking about Elder Perrault, dreaming of the day when he would just be plain old Jean-Marc.

"You don't have to give me notice," Marguerite said cheerfully when I told her of my father's offer. "I've been waiting for a chance to introduce my niece, Colette, to the gospel, and now I could call her and say that I'm desperate for her. She's not expecting her first baby until the end of next month, so we'll have plenty of time to find a replacement for you." She hugged me suddenly. "But that doesn't mean I'm not going to miss you terribly. You're like a daughter to me." She stopped to wipe a tear from her eye with the back of her rough hand.

"And don't worry about your apartment. The people the missionaries were living with had a new baby and want to use the missionaries' room for a nursery. They came by last night and told me, so I said they could rent your old apartment. Someone in the ward has already donated twin beds and a couch. With the furniture you left, they'll have things pretty good—for missionaries." She laughed. "So I'll give you back two weeks' rent for this month to go for your mission. They'll be moving in this afternoon, if it's all right with you."

Things were working out wonderfully. "That's great! But I still have a few things I forgot, pictures and stuff."

"Well, you can run up and get those things after the lunch rush."

The afternoon sped by as we helped and laughed with the customers. During a brief lull, Marguerite called Colette, who promised to be there the very next day. I had a bittersweet feeling, knowing everything I did that day at the cafe was for the last time. I had many good memories there.

Finally, things slowed down during the late afternoon. "Why don't you go now?" Marguerite asked.

I glanced around the nearly deserted cafe. "Okay. I'll be back in a few minutes. It shouldn't take me long."

Marguerite shrugged. "Take as long as you want."

The hall was strangely quiet as I made my way to my old apartment. Memories of Nette and days gone by fluttered through my mind like the ghosts they were. But I felt no regret at leaving. I had to go on with my life.

The door was slightly ajar when I arrived. It seemed the missionaries were already moving in. "Hello?" I called.

"Come on in," someone said. So I pushed the door open and walked in.

"Surprise!" yelled many voices as I sat there blinking in surprise. "Happy Birthday!"

I laughed. I had completely forgotten it was my birthday. Everyone close to me in the ward was there, as were my parents. There were so many people in the room that I practically had to squeeze my way into the apartment. The small kitchen table had been dragged to the center of the room and, along with the coffee table, was loaded with treats.

Marguerite arrived shortly after me with additional food and drinks from the cafe. "Don't worry about going back to the cafe tonight," she said. "I got Dauphine to cover for you. I'm going to stay with you myself until the dinner rush begins."

It was a birthday party like I had known only when Antoine was alive, and I found myself laughing and talking as I hadn't for years. I received many presents, mostly books and church-related items. Towards the end, when people started leaving, the elders finally showed up, carrying their suitcases.

"You're a little late," I teased.

"Yes, we know," Elder Perrault rejoined. "But it's your fault."

"What?"

"Some lawyer called us this morning and asked to see us this afternoon. He said he was the one who prosecuted Jacques' case a year and a half ago. We've just spent hours in a first discussion with him and his family." He shook his head in amazement. "You never cease to surprise me, Ari."

At his use of my nickname, my mother looked up quickly. But during the week I had grown used to him calling me that. In fact, I loved hearing it said in his caressing voice.

"These are the elders, Mother, Father. They're the missionaries in this area. I'm going to be doing what they're doing," I said.

"What is it exactly that you do?" my father asked. Elder Jones immediately began explaining.

Seeing that his companion had things well under control, Elder Perrault picked up the luggage. "Which way to the bedroom?" I pointed it out, and even walked over with him to open the door. He smiled his thanks and went inside as I returned to the living room to listen to Elder Jones, my parents, and the few remaining party guests discuss missionary life.

Through the open bedroom door I could see Elder Perrault unpacking his suitcase, putting most of his clothing on hangers in the closet. I saw him take something else out of his suitcase and slide it under one of the twin beds. But not before I had seen what it was—a poster of me from the Coalition's campaign. *Why does he have that?* I asked myself hopefully. A warm feeling spread over me.

"Ariana." My mother's voice called to me as if from far away. "Are you ready to go home?"

"Uh, yeah. I've just got to get my pictures." I went around the room quickly, taking down the few pictures I wanted to keep. I handed them to my mother.

"Is that all?"

I shook my head. "I've got a few more in the bedroom. One more of Nette and one of me." I turned to go into the bedroom, but stopped at the door. Elder Perrault had taken down the photograph of me from the wall and was staring at it. One hand reached out to touch the glass, as if stroking my face. I coughed delicately and he started. He looked up and our eyes met. We stood there not speaking, as a current of something wonderful and priceless seemed to pass through us.

He spoke, his voice suddenly husky. "You left this, Ari." He came across the room to give it to me. "And this one as well." He took a picture of Nette off the dresser near the door. "This is a very good picture of you," he said, indicating the first one. As he talked, his companion and my parents came over to look at it. The strange intensity of my emotions made me glad they had come. I knew Elder Perrault would never do anything to jeopardize his missionary status, but I didn't have the same confidence in myself. At least not when I felt the way I did at that moment.

"Here."

I accepted the picture from Elder Perrault's reluctant hands. Was I only imagining his reluctance? "Thanks," I said. "Monique took it, and she liked it so much that she had it enlarged and put in a frame to give me for Christmas." Looking at his familiar face, I added impulsively, "Would you like to keep it, Elder Perrault?"

His eyes told me how much he did before he spoke. "I would, Ari. It'll be a great remembrance of our most successful missionary team member. Right, Elder Jones?" He glanced over at his companion who nodded.

We said our goodbyes, and on the way home I was very quiet. I wasn't sad, only aware of my budding feelings for Elder Perrault. Somehow I knew he was very special.

Three weeks after my birthday, I received my mission call. I was called to the Bordeaux mission, due to leave the first of May, three weeks away.

"Only three weeks?" my mother asked when I told my parents.

I smiled. "That only means I'll be home sooner," I replied.

"I know." My mother sniffed and reached out to hug me. Her embrace was just what I needed. I felt loved and happy.

The weeks passed by quickly. I enjoyed both school and my new job immensely. Spring was beautiful, and I found myself taking walks again along the Seine, contemplating my life. Compared to where I had come from, it seemed nearly perfect. I was so excited to serve a mission! A week before I left, I received my endowments at the temple in Switzerland. To my joy, while in the temple I felt I could almost glimpse beyond the veil to see my baby.

With a rapidity that scared me, Saturday night arrived, two days before I was due to leave. My mother and I were packing my clothes into two suitcases. Most of the items were new and in very good taste, all picked out and paid for by my mother.

"Does this go?" she asked, pointing to a picture of Nette on my dresser.

"No. I already have tons of them in my suitcase. I'll leave that one for you."

"Thanks," she said quietly, holding the photograph to her slim body. She turned her gaze on me intently, as if searching. "Do you . . ." she began hesitantly. "Do you ever wish you could go back and change things so that those years after Antoine's death had never happened?"

I shook my head violently. "Never! Not ever! That would mean Nette would never have existed. And I could never wish for that."

"Yes," she nodded. "That's how I feel. Even though Antoine's death hurt us all, I never could wish that he had never existed."

We stared at each other, caught up in our thoughts. We had both been through the worst a mother could face and had survived, though not unmarked. Of the two of us, I was better off; I at least had hope for the future, while my mother did not.

The next day at church, I said goodbye to all my friends. There was a flurry of address exchanging and hugs and kisses. Marguerite was especially emotional. "Thanks so much for everything," she said.

"No, I should thank you," I returned.

But she shook her head. "I mean for introducing us to the Church. Now it looks as though Colette and her husband will be baptized, and my sister is even taking the discussions." I could hardly picture the large, terse-faced Françoise agreeing to listen to the missionaries, but I was happy for her. I was even more excited to know that Colette was accepting the gospel. She had returned home about the time I had received my mission call and I had not had word of her since, except that she had given birth to a healthy baby boy.

"I'm so glad!" I hugged Marguerite and Jules both.

A cough sounded behind us. I turned around to see Elder Perrault and Elder Jones.

"I've got something for you, Ari." Elder Perrault held out a paper in his hand.

"What is it?" I asked as I reached for it, but I immediately saw that it was a list of ten names.

He grinned. "Well, your mission covers where I live, and just in case you serve anywhere near my home, I've written down the names of ten people for you to go and see. You did it for me, so I want to do it for you. I've been writing to these people and preparing them since I've been on my mission."

"Well, thanks," I said. "But I never did give you ten names, you know."

He looked at me seriously. "You're only one short." He motioned to his companion, who took a paper out of his notebook. "We've decided to give it back to you until you finish it. If not for us, then for the other missionaries who follow." I took the proffered sheet and saw that someone had written in my parents' names. Now only one space was left blank.

"Thanks." I put both papers carefully away and turned to leave the building. Outside, clouds had gathered, blotting out the sun. I sighed in frustration. After weeks of beautiful sunshine and warmth, the rain had chosen this day to return.

I glanced back to see Elder Perrault watching me. "You'll write?" I asked.

"I will write, Ari," he said softly. "And please believe me when I say that someday the rain will remind you of Nette and Antoine, without the pain."

Once again I heard the promise in his voice.

CHAPTER THIRTEEN

I had been away from home several weeks when I received Jean-Marc's first letter. It was mid-May, warm and sunny, with only occasional rain showers to remind me of my past. I was serving in Tours at the time, feeling homesick and sort of lost, and I tore the envelope open greedily.

My dearest Ari,

How wonderful it is to write to you and to finally share my feelings without fear of breaking any rules. Though you are far away from me, I feel closer to you since I can write. Aren't we lucky not to be serving in the same mission?

I did not write to you before now to give you a chance to settle into your mission life. Also I was transferred to LeHavre and have been very busy myself, reopening an area here and training a very green American. But beginning today, I will write to you weekly as I promised.

I am pleasantly plagued with thoughts of you daily, and finally I can tell you so. It's time I risked my feelings (and your possible rejection) and confessed that I have felt something special for you since I first saw your commercial over a year and a half ago. It touched me in a way I can't describe. I wanted to hold and love and comfort you. I did some checking and found that you lived in Paris, though I never dreamed you were a member. When I was called to serve in the Paris mission, I brought my poster of you, knowing somehow we would meet.

And we did! What a wonderful day for me! The fact that you were already a member only made me even more sure that you were as special as I had thought. As we started to work together on the missionary team, my feelings for you grew—first as a friend, and then . . . Well, I didn't dare think beyond that, except to begin praying that you would go on a mission so I could at least have a chance with you when my service is over.

It's raining here as I write this, and Ari, I love the rain because it reminds me of you. I hope you will also think of me when it rains, and not just of sad things. If you give me a chance, I promise someday I will help you love the rain.

Write to me soon.

Yours, Elder Jean-Marc Perrault.

P.S. Your lawyer friend, his wife, and their three children were baptized yesterday by Elder Jones and his new companion! He called and asked me to tell you thanks for your great example. He will be a bishop one day, I think.

P.P.S. I'm glad you think I am similar to your brother, but don't ever make the mistake of thinking my feelings for you are brotherly!

I laughed with joy and even cried a bit. His feelings for me were all I could hope for at the moment. The next preparation day I wrote him a long letter, recounting everything I had been doing and how much his letter meant to me. I also admitted my feelings for him. Thus began a year and a half of weekly letters. With each long letter, my love for him grew. I learned about him, about things I had only suspected before. I found he shared my love of numbers, of rivers, and of watching people. And most importantly, we had the same eternal goals.

But that was only the beginning of what I would learn about my Jean-Marc.

I had been out in the mission field a year when I found I was to be transferred in a week to Bordeaux, and I would serve in Jean-Marc's home ward. He was thrilled. "Go see my family, lovely Ari," he wrote. "I've told them all about you. They will make great members of a missionary team. Show them my list of people, and tell them I said they'd help."

I was transferred on a Monday, and that night my junior companion, Sister Moura from Portugal, and I went to see the family, armed with Jean-Marc's list. My companion had been in the area two months, and knew them well.

I felt nervous as we rang the outside bell to their apartment. "Who is it?" they asked through the speaker.

"The sisters," my companion answered. The buzzer sounded, and soon we were on our way up the elevator.

"This is my new companion," Sister Moura said as we were ushered into a modest apartment by a plump woman and a thin girl of about sixteen. "She knew your son in Paris. Her name is Sister Ariana Merson." I had taken back my maiden name after my divorce.

Jean-Marc's mother stared at me incredulously. "You mean you're Jean-Marc's Ari? How glad I am to meet you at last!" She hugged me effusively, then settled me down on her flowered sofa. "You may call me Louise, and this is my daughter, Lu-Lu." She indicated the young girl. "Jean-Marc's brother is working at our store. You knew we had a grocery store, didn't you?" I nodded. Jean-Marc had mentioned it in his letters. "Now tell me, how did you and Jean-Marc meet?"

I was swept up instantly by Louise's warmth and charm, and soon I was telling her of my time with Jean-Marc in Paris. When I was finished, she sighed heavily. "Yes, that is what he told me. Ah, that boy has been a blessing to me, he really has, and I miss him every day." She straightened up on her chair, flashing me a smile much like Jean-Marc's. "But I know he is in the service of the Lord, and that is what is important. And to think he met you as he dreamed of doing since your commercial came out on TV! And you a member; that is a miracle indeed."

She paused a moment, and I sat there with a silly smile on my face, suddenly speechless. What does one say to the mother of the man she loves? I turned my head to look around the comfortable room, especially noticing the photographs lining her piano in the corner of the room. Impulsively, I got up to examine them.

"Did Jean-Marc tell you why he is older than the other mission-aries?" Louise asked suddenly. I turned from the many pictures of

Jean-Marc and his siblings and shook my head. I had been curious, but I hadn't yet asked him about it. After what was in my own past, I didn't feel I had to judge what he might have been—only what he now was.

"I thought not," she went on. "You see, Jean-Marc's brother, Pierre, is just a year older than he is, and they have both worked for me at the store since they were little. Their father died when Lu-Lu was still a baby, shortly after we joined the Church. At first, other family members helped me with the store, but finally my boys were old enough to do the work. And by the time Pierre went on his mission, Lu-Lu also could help. So Pierre left with the understanding that Jean-Marc would stay behind to help us with the store until he got back. Then Jean-Marc would go while Pierre stayed with us. That would put Jean-Marc on his mission only a year after the other boys his age.

"When Pierre finally got home, Jean-Marc started his mission papers, but the army got him first," she continued. I nodded. Every young man in France was required to serve almost a year in the army. "You see, Pierre had gotten deferment while on his mission, and afterwards applied for the family dependent exemption so as not to leave me alone with the store. Jean-Marc had applied for a temporary exemption while Pierre was away, and then tried to get a deferment for his mission, but they did not accept it." She shook her head somewhat angrily. "The man who reviewed Jean-Marc's petition used to be an old friend of our family, but he wouldn't have anything to do with us once we were baptized. I think it was because of this that he refused deferment to Jean-Marc."

"How frustrating!" I exclaimed.

Louise nodded, coming to stand beside the piano. "But Jean-Marc took it all in stride. He didn't let it get him down. He said there must have been a reason for the delay, and that he had to have trust in the Lord. He has always been a good example to us."

"That was about the same time the sister's commercial came out, wasn't it, Mother?" Lu-Lu spoke for the first time. The green-brown eyes that were twins to Jean-Marc's watched me intently.

Louise nodded, tracing a finger along the frame of a recent picture of Jean-Marc. She glanced up. "Yes. He had a poster of you in his room. He said he was going to find you and baptize you someday, that there was something different about you." Her voice grew quiet. "You know, he really loves you. In his last letter, he said he feels sure the Lord delayed his mission so he could meet you. And from all he's told me, I think he was right."

"He never told me," I said softly. I was happy to hear her words, but I suddenly felt very uncomfortable. I looked to my companion for help.

"Show them the list, Sister," she said helpfully.

"Oh, yes." I crossed to the couch to pick up my appointment book. Carefully tucked into the flap at the back were the two papers Jean-Marc had given me that last Sunday—the two lists of names, one mine and one his. I drew his out and showed it to Louise.

She smiled. "Yes, he told me about this list and who was on it," she said as she held it in her hands. "The first person is Elisabeth, our next-door neighbor. For two years I have been trying to send her the missionaries, and she has always refused."

I was puzzled. "Then why does Jean-Marc think she will accept me?"

Her eyes met mine. "If she ever would accept a missionary, it would be you," she replied enigmatically. She crossed the room to the couch and sat down with the others.

"Why me?" I asked.

But it was Lu-Lu who answered. "It's because of your commercials and posters." That explained somewhat. Often during my mission, people had been curious about my past and it had led to discussions, especially these last few months as they had begun to play my commercials again after nine months of having focused on other similar commercials. Marie, the lady in charge of my campaign, had written to tell me that mine had been the most successful, so they were giving them another try.

Louise sighed. "You see, Elisabeth lost a baby two years ago in a car accident, shortly after she moved here. She hasn't been the same since."

Understanding dawned. I too had lost a baby, and maybe I could give this woman hope where no one else had been able to. "Well," I said softly, "I'm willing to give it a try." I gazed down again at the photographs of Jean-Marc. A fresh May breeze came through the window and touched my face like a whisper or a caress. *I will try my best, Jean-Marc,* I thought silently. Aloud I said, "Can we go now?"

The others looked at me, startled. "Right now?" asked Louise.

I shrugged. "She'll either accept or she won't. I feel we should go now." Hope flashed briefly over Louise's face, and I felt myself drawn to this woman who cared so deeply about her neighbor. *Jean-Marc is very lucky to have such a mother,* I thought.

I could see that my companion was nervous. I, too, felt my stomach churning. To hold the salvation of another person in one's hands was almost too much to bear, even if only temporarily. *Please, Father,* I prayed. *Let me be enough to get her to listen. Let Nette's death be worth this one thing more.* As I prayed, longing for my baby came over me and I almost wept. I shut my eyes momentarily against the pain, knowing that it would abate.

But it didn't. We were at the Elisabeth's door now, and it was as if my emptiness and longing grew by the moment. The grief I felt seemed fresh. *Why, Father?* I pleaded. But then I knew I was being reminded of my loss distinctly so I could understand how real it still was for this woman who didn't have the gospel to help her understand her devastating loss.

Louise rang the bell but didn't back off as I had expected. She stayed in front of me with a determined expression on her face. I was glad, because I wasn't sure if I would be able to speak past the bitter lump of sorrow forming in my throat.

"Oh, hi, Louise," said the woman who opened the door, as she looked up at the taller Louise. I knew instinctively that this was Elisabeth. She was young, maybe five years older than myself. She wasn't slim, but not fat either, and with her dark eyes and auburn hair, she was very pretty. She appeared to be a normal woman, except for her eyes, which had the same hopelessness mine had held before I had joined the Church—empty, longing, alone, and so afraid of trying again.

"I have someone I want you to meet, Elisabeth," Louise said softly in the stillness of the hallway. "Jean-Marc sent her to you." Louise's hand reached out, lightning quick, and squeezed mine reassuringly. Then she moved her bulky figure to the side, and I faced

Elisabeth alone.

Her eyes focused on my name tag first. "Louise, we have gone over this," she began, but suddenly she saw my face and stopped talking. She gasped. "The girl on Jean-Marc's poster, the one whose baby died!" Her eyes began to water. "You're a member of their church? But how? Why? How can you serve God after what he did to you?"

I met her gaze steadily, seeing the anguish in her face, and I couldn't help the genuine tears that fell from my eyes and onto my cheeks. "Because," I said softly, remembering the thing that had bothered me most once I had begun to believe in a heaven, "I know where my baby is, and who is holding and loving and singing to her. May I please come in so that I can tell you about it?" As I spoke, a vision of Elder Tarr standing in the poorly-lit corridor outside the apartment Nette and I had shared passed through my mind. Now I knew how he felt that day two and a half years ago—anxious, hoping, fearful, accountable, and loving. How could I love this woman I had never before met? Why had Elder Tarr loved me? I knew the answer, of course, being a missionary and having felt the pure love of Christ before. But each time the feeling came as a new wonder.

She stared at me, and for a long moment our souls communicated; we were bonded by our loss. Then, "Yes," she said in a whisper, full of hope and longing. "Please. Oh, please come in."

CHAPTER FOURTEEN

The July day was hot and sweltering, but my companion and I didn't notice the heat. With smiles on our lips and a song in our hearts we made our way from the church to Louise's apartment, where an informal gathering was celebrating our ward's latest converts, Elisabeth and her husband, René. They had been baptized only that day by Pierre, Louise's oldest son, Jean-Marc's brother.

It had been a long two months of working with them, of weaving the discussions into my story so they would listen. Getting Elisabeth to pray had been the most difficult, but her husband's eager willingness to do anything at all that might bring his beloved wife back to herself helped things along. Many days Elisabeth and I had simply cried together. But finally, she gained a testimony for herself and had begun to live again, even thinking of having another child one day—something her husband had been urging, but that she had utterly refused to consider. "To bring another child into the world so that God can take it away?" she had said contemptuously the first time I had brought it up. But gradually her misplaced anger at the Lord grew into acceptance and even understanding. She began to smile and read the Book of Mormon, and at last had asked to be baptized.

"Thank you, Sister Merson," she had said afterwards. "I can never thank you enough for giving my baby boy back to me again, and my husband, and my faith." I had hugged her and cried, not knowing how to tell her that I hadn't done anything someone hadn't already done for me.

My companion, a new one since Sister Moura had been transferred only last week, and I were a little late to the baptismal party
because of the next three people on Jean-Marc's list. They were all
young, single people from Jean-Marc's school days, and we had
brought them to see the baptisms. Afterward they had many
questions for us, so we had stayed to teach them. We had been
impressed to challenge them to be baptized, and two had immediately accepted. I felt the third would soon follow.

On the way to Louise's apartment, I was thinking about the long
letter I would write to Jean-Marc the next preparation day when I
saw a scrawny figure slumped, unseeing, against an apartment
building near Louise's. From the looks of the thin legs jutting out at
odd angles from the rag-clothed torso, I knew it was a woman. She
had her head thrown back against the wall, her dull brown hair swept
up and over to cover her face entirely, dirty arms limply dangling,
fingers with broken nails caught between loose cobblestones on the
sidewalk.

We stopped and stared, as did several other people. It was a
repulsive sight, and part of me wanted to flee. Yet somehow, the
figure was strangely familiar. People shifted uncomfortably in the hot
sun. A sight such as this was familiar to some, but certainly not on
this side of town.

"Go call the police," said one man somewhat tersely.

"Yeah, we don't want any whores around here," said another next
to him.

"She needs help," I heard myself saying. I drew closer to the
sprawled figure, glancing only once at my junior companion, Sister
Osborne, who followed somewhat nervously.

"Be careful, girl," warned the first man. "These people are
sometimes dangerous."

"And you might catch something," murmured the second man,
almost under his breath.

I was standing beside the woman now, and gingerly pushed back
her hair. I gasped in shock.

"Paulette!"

I was kneeling beside her in an instant, shaking her and trying to wake her. When my efforts failed, I simply hugged her tightly.

"Is she dead?" the first man asked.

I shook my head. "Unconscious."

"You know her?"

I nodded. "She was my best friend—once. She needs a doctor." I peered up at the two men who had come closer, pleading. "Please, will you help me? There's a doctor nearby, a friend of mine." Even though Paulette looked thin, she was dead weight. There was no way I could get her back to the apartment alone, and my companion wouldn't be much help because of all our books and discussion guides.

"Not me," said the second man, backing away.

The other man regarded me intently for a moment. "Hey, you're the girl on that drug commercial, aren't you?"

"Yes, that's me. Will you help me?"

"Yes, I will," he said. "I'd do just about anything for you. Your commercial helped me get my own daughter off drugs." He bent to pick up Paulette, while I reached for the dirty duffle bag that was half under her.

"Thanks." I cast a hard glance at the second man who had refused to help, but he and the others were already moving away to find something else to do with their lives.

"Is that from your drug organization?" the man asked me, motioning to my name tag.

So I began to explain about the Church, about how I joined and what I had been doing since. When I was finished, the man smiled at me for the first time. "It sounds as though your church is something my daughter needs. Maybe you could come by and meet her."

I couldn't believe my ears. It seemed as though the promise our mission president had made to us was coming true: "People are out there waiting to be baptized. They are practically falling out of the sky and into the baptismal font. Keep the mission rules, pray hard, and most of all, open your mouths and people will find you."

We took Paulette to Louise's, where the party was in full swing. At Louise's insistence, the man who carried her stayed for refreshments. I asked Lu-Lu to be a temporary companion to Sister Osborne and help her watch over the man who unknowingly had just become our newest investigator. Then I went into the back bedroom where Louise, Elisabeth, and René were standing over Paulette.

Now, I had exaggerated when I said that I knew a doctor. René was only studying to become one, and still had years left to complete his studies. But he had always planned to specialize in drug rehabilitation, so I figured he must know something.

"Will she be all right?" I asked.

He sighed. "I don't know, Sister." He pulled up her sleeve and showed me the needle tracks on her arm. "I mean, she'll come out of it this time, but the next she may not be so lucky. She'll have severe withdrawal symptoms, and there's nothing we can give her that will dim the cravings. She'll do almost anything to get drugs. It's my bet that she's already done things she never dreamed of doing."

I knew he was talking about prostitution, and I looked down on my once-best friend sadly. "Isn't there anything we can do for her?" Even my time on the drug hotline hadn't prepared me for this. Mostly I had talked to depressed teenagers who were thinking about doing drugs, not ones who were truly addicted.

"Yes, we can keep her away from drugs," René said. "But none of us has the money to put her into one of those fancy programs, and the free ones don't have the constant supervision she will need until she's stronger. That is, assuming she even wants to be free of the drugs."

"We can do it," said Louise without hesitation. "We can get volunteers from the ward to stay with her while we're working, and she can sleep here." Her voice was firm. "Don't worry, Ari," she added softly, for the first time forgetting my missionary title. "We'll help your friend, won't we, Elisabeth?"

Elisabeth nodded. "Remember, you told me that's what a ward was for—to help each other. I'll take a shift with her each day after work. And René will be our medical advisor."

"We'll start with volunteers from the party." Louise was already out the door, followed by the other two.

I stayed behind to study Paulette's lifeless face, the lavish makeup smeared, a blackening bruise covering one side. She looked so old and ravaged. "This is partly my fault," I whispered to her, remembering the many times she had come to the cafe to play with Nette. "I never told you that I forgave you. I never even imagined how you must have suffered with Nette's death. I'm so sorry." I bent down to kiss her pale cheek.

Paulette didn't wake until late the next afternoon. Lu-Lu and another girl in the ward were with her. They helped her bathe and dress and fixed her something to eat, all the while talking and laughing like the youngsters they were. I had been calling after every teaching appointment to see if she was yet awake. Finally Lu-Lu announced that she had awakened, and she wanted to see me.

We had just finished giving the first discussion to the man who had helped us with Paulette. He, his wife, and two daughters seemed very open and willing to learn. The daughters even offered to take turns sitting with Paulette when they heard what had happened. After our lesson, they let me use their phone to call and see if she was awake.

"We'll be right there, Lu-Lu!" I practically yelled into the phone. I turned to the others. "She's awake. We'll let you know what happens." In seconds we were out the door and waiting to catch a bus to Louise's apartment.

Paulette was on the flowered couch in the sitting room when we arrived. She looked impossibly thin and somewhat rebellious. "The girls say I can't leave without them," she remarked. "Am I a prisoner here, or what?"

I smiled. "Don't be ridiculous. We just want to take care of you for awhile. Will you stay?"

A tired expression came over Paulette's face. "Yes, I'll stay—for now. But I'm not promising anything, Ariana."

"I want you to promise me one thing." I crossed over to sit with her on the couch. "That before you leave, you'll say goodbye. You didn't the last time, you know."

"You didn't either," she muttered evasively.

"I know, and I'm sorry." For a moment she seemed close to tears. I reached over to hug her. "I love you, you know," I whispered. She didn't reply.

The shakes started the next day. By the time I saw her again in the evening, she was nervous, hyper, and unsteady as her body cried out for the drugs she was used to. She talked too fast, didn't listen to what was being said, and was rude to those who reached out to help. But the many volunteers had been warned, and they came prepared with iron-clad feelings and projects that might keep Paulette's thoughts off drugs. The young adults in the ward took her to activities, service projects, and even home to their own families. I was continually amazed at their dedication.

But despite their help and our first successful week of keeping Paulette off drugs, I knew we weren't going to make it. Everyone was working for Paulette except for Paulette. She kept talking about leaving, about finding something to relieve her tension—drugs. Yet, she didn't go. I wasn't sure why until we stopped by on Saturday morning.

The door to Louise's apartment was opened by Pierre, Jean-Marc's brother. He looked a great deal like Jean-Marc, and every time I saw him my heart leapt, though when he spoke, it was clear he wasn't the man whose letters were making me love him more each week.

"Sisters! I'm so glad you're here!" Pierre's honest face was a mask of relief. "Elisabeth was supposed to be staying with Paulette, but she's gone. I don't know what happened. I was in the sitting room with Paulette, talking about her past—I thought it would help her to understand why she got so involved with drugs in the first place— and Elisabeth was in the kitchen listening to us, but she suddenly left. I went and knocked on her door and she wouldn't answer, but I know she's in there. Now I'm late for the store, and Saturday's our biggest day. I've called a few people, but no one's home or they can't come to sit with Paulette. But that's not the worst thing. Paulette says she's leaving now. She's packing that dingy old bag she has with the clothes we all gave her, and now she's leaving! Can you stop her?" He stopped finally, the rush of words ended. I watched him curiously. For some reason he was very upset by Paulette's pending departure, much more than I would have thought. Of course he had been spending a lot of time with her, as had Elisabeth. . . .

Thinking of Elisabeth brought me abruptly around. As a very new member whose testimony was still fragile, she had to be my first concern. "Okay, we'll go talk to Elisabeth, quickly, just for a minute.

Then we'll come and stay with Paulette while you go to work—if I can get her to stay—and if we can't find anyone to come and stay with her, we'll take her proselyting."

Pierre blinked once or twice at that, then smiled the endearing grin he shared with his brother. "I like that idea." We all laughed.

"Now don't let her leave, Pierre," I said. "Tell her she promised to say goodbye to me." He nodded, and we turned and headed down the hall to Elisabeth's. She opened the door on the very first ring, as if she had been waiting for us.

"I saw you through the peephole," she admitted. "I was trying to decide whether or not to go back to Paulette when you came." She began to wring her hands as she talked, glancing around her small entryway, avoiding our eyes.

"What happened?" Sister Osborne asked.

Elisabeth sighed and looked at the ceiling, blinking rapidly to stop the forming tears from falling. "They were talking, Paulette and Pierre, about what happened before she came here, how she used to do drugs, but how after your baby died she went totally crazy. She said that for a long time, she didn't even know what town she was in or where she was sleeping. Just a blur, she said. But the part that got me was where she sat and watched your husband give drugs to that tiny little baby without stopping him. I suddenly couldn't stand to be around a person who could sit and watch a baby die! I can't believe I even spent so much time with her this week—I feel sick when I think about it!" She glared at me defiantly, but I only nodded in understanding. I, too, had hated Paulette for what she had done—until I had seen her sprawled on the sidewalk nearly a week before. I didn't know exactly what changed me or when it had happened, but I didn't blame Paulette anymore.

Then Elisabeth asked the question I knew was coming. "How can you stand to help a person who did that to your baby? I don't think I could do it. If the person who killed my baby hadn't also died in the car accident, I think I would hate him still!"

I blinked and took a big breath before replying. "I hated Paulette for a long time—blamed her, even. But you don't know how my ex-husband is—he could charm a hare right out of the paws of a hungry lion. He did it, not Paulette. She was even under the influence of drugs at the time it happened. She did try to stop him, and she called the police. But all that doesn't matter, not really. The fact is that she is repentant; and no one, not you, not me, can judge her or say that Jesus' atonement doesn't apply to her." Until I said the words, I hadn't realized I felt them that strongly. "Jesus loves Paulette just as much as he loves us. We have to forgive her. Remember that by the same spirit we judge and forgive, we will be judged and forgiven. See if you can't find it within yourself to forgive Paulette. She needs us now, and I know she has become especially attached to you. I'm afraid that without all of us, we will lose her."

I hugged her, but she didn't return the embrace. "We'll be over at Louise's if you change your mind," I added softly. "I hope you come." My companion and I were silent as we made our way quickly back to Louise's.

"Thanks," Pierre said as he left, pausing at the door to cast a pleading glance at Paulette. "Please be here when I come back." She shook her head violently, but he was already out the door.

"Don't try and stop me, Ariana." Paulette picked up her duffle bag. Her hands were shaking and I could tell she was suffering more withdrawal pains, maybe not as severe as before, but still very real and compelling.

Our eyes met from across the entryway, hers looking so scared and young without her mask of makeup. "Were you going to leave without saying goodbye?"

She shrugged indifferently. "You're the only reason I've stayed as long as I have—you and Pierre. But I didn't think you would want me to say goodbye under the circumstances."

That made me angry. "What circumstances—because you're going to get a fix? Do you think I don't know what you're feeling? Maybe not exactly, but I do know that you're suffering! Your face is haggard, you've got the shakes, and you are downright rude! But everyone here has opened their hearts to you, given you a place to stay, helped you. Everyone except you, Paulette. It all comes down to you in the end. What do you want to do with the rest of your life? Do you even *want* a life?" I shook my head slowly. "No, that's it, isn't it? You don't even want to live. You don't care about any of us."

She didn't reply, but dropped her gaze. I moved closer to her, fighting to contain my desire to shake her. "Paulette, look at me! Can you at least tell me why? I know it's hard, but with so much help, you could beat the drugs. Tell me, why quit now?" Tears flooded my eyes.

Paulette clenched her jaw, and for a moment I thought she would flee, but she didn't. "It's you, Ariana. I keep seeing your face the night Nette died, and knowing that I was responsible. Every day here you have come to see me, and I see your pain again, and I don't know how you can ever forgive me for what I've done!" She began to sob and I reached out, not to shake, but to hug my friend.

"But it wasn't your fault, Paulette. And I did forgive you. It took a long time, but I don't blame you anymore. And now you've got to forgive yourself. I know for me, that took even longer." I held her back to stare into her eyes again. "But look at my face now. Do you see pain, unhappiness, anger? I hope you don't, because that's all gone now, since I've accepted the truth. Take a good look at me." She did as I asked, and abruptly stopped crying.

"Paulette, we are much more than we seem. We are eternal creatures, and we have to see things with an eternal perspective. Nette's not gone forever. Haven't you heard any of what we've talked about each time I've visited you this week? The plan of our Father in Heaven allows for families to be together forever, despite death. One day we will both see little Nette, clothed in all the robes of a princess in heaven."

"You really believe that?" Paulette asked hesitantly, afraid to hope. "Nette's still alive somewhere, waiting for you?"

"I do. And you can know for yourself that it's true. God loves you every bit as much as he loves me!"

"But I've done so much wrong since Nette died," she said earnestly. The regret in her voice cut deep into my heart. "Things to earn money for drugs. I've about done it all."

We began to teach Paulette about repentance, my companion and I, slipping easily into our role as missionaries. Finally, Paulette was open to our teachings, and I knew that she was hearing them for the first time, though we'd already talked about them earlier in the week. It was as if my verbal forgiveness, and her seeing my face without pain, reached the place deep inside her that still wanted to try.

After a long time we got up to leave, already late for our morning street meeting with the other missionaries in our zone, planned for the flea market nearby. Paulette agreed to go with us. We met Elisabeth at the door, her eyes red and tearful.

"I'm sorry," she said. "You are right, Sister. Paulette, can you ever forgive me?"

Paulette was genuinely puzzled. "For what?"

"Never mind," Elisabeth smiled, knowing instinctively that to tell her would only reopen her barely-closing wounds. "But René and I were talking yesterday, and we want to know if you would like to stay with us until you're completely back on your feet, and maybe longer. Louise doesn't have as much room as we do, and it's not proper for you to stay in their house with Pierre feeling the way he does about you." At her words Paulette reddened, and I laughed. I was not the only one, it seemed, who had noticed Pierre's devotion to Paulette. "Anyway, Louise and Pierre always need a hand at the store, so they'll give you a job—they've asked already, haven't they? I thought so. Well, what do you think?"

We all knew that what Elisabeth was really asking was if Paulette was going to stay and kick the drug habit that had imprisoned her for so long. If she was going to let us love her.

Paulette was quiet for a long time and then she nodded, meeting Elisabeth's eyes. "Yes. I want to stay with you, if you really mean it."

Elisabeth hugged her. "Oh, I do."

Even though Elisabeth had forgiven Paulette and everything was happy again, they both ended up going with us to the street meeting. Paulette had never seen one before and was curious. We even got them to sing with some of the missionaries and hold up signs while we contacted people in the streets. When I glanced at Paulette a short time later, I could see the happiness on her face and knew she was going to make it.

Two months later I was transferred, just a week after Paulette's baptism and engagement to Pierre. Sister Osborne and I had only baptized two-thirds of Jean-Marc's list, though we had contacted all of them. I left the list for her to finish. As I took it out to give her, I noticed my own list with the last number still blank. *Should I fill in*

Paulette's name? I asked myself. But something stopped me. Somehow I didn't feel that last name would be so easy.

Once I was settled in my new area, Elisabeth wrote to tell me she was expecting another baby. "I'm almost scared to love it when I remember what happened to my first child," she wrote. "But knowing I will have my little boy again someday gives me the courage to love again. Indeed, I already love this baby with an intensity I didn't believe I'd ever feel again. Thank you so much for everything. And one more thing: if the baby is a girl, I'm going to name her after you."

Paulette also wrote to me, though her letters were rare and very short. But she was drug-free, in love, and happy again—and that's all that mattered.

I served the last two months of my mission in Nantes. As the end of my service approached, I felt excited and scared all at once. Jean-Marc would be transferred home a week after I got off my mission. That left one Sunday to see him before he went home. He had been transferred back into the same zone he'd been in when I left, though not the same area or ward, and would be at the baptismal meeting on Sunday since the zone baptisms were always held in our chapel.

In my mind I imagined the conversations we might have, the feelings our hearts would feel, the expressions our faces would show. But nothing, I knew, would equal the real thing.

CHAPTER FIFTEEN

Fog, deep and dark like a heavy blanket in winter, covered Paris in the early mornings of late October. I didn't mind. It was a lot better than the rain and the fading memories it still brought to mind.

I had settled happily into my parents' apartment and was savoring their pampering. Father insisted I take a week off before returning to the bank, and Mother enjoyed herself thoroughly by giving away my worn missionary clothing and buying new things. I spent the foggy mornings sleeping in and dreaming of my promising future with Jean-Marc. The days I spent visiting friends, reading, or writing letters. I also organized my mission mementos, putting pictures in albums and throwing away papers that no longer had any meaning. In the cleaning out I came across my list of ten people, already yellowing and torn in several spots. The last name was still blank. I felt the urge to throw the list away—hadn't I already done my share? But I knew that though my mission was over, my life's mission had just begun. And I would start that service by filling in that last name—when I could think of someone. Smiling, I slipped the sheet into the extra Book of Mormon I always carried in my purse or briefcase.

The first friends I visited were Marguerite and Jules. They were doing so well at the cafe that they had opened a second one; Colette and her husband, who had both been long baptized, were managing it. The missionaries still lived in Marguerite's building, and the cafe had become a great contact place for them as well as a hangout for ward youth.

I looked up other friends—even Monique, who had since married and moved to another city and ward. She was now expecting her first baby. I was happy for her, happy for all my friends whose lives had gone on while I had put mine on hold for a mission. I missed the way things had been, but I was too excited about my own love for Jean-Marc to begrudge them their new lives and loves.

Sunday morning, I went to church and spoke in sacrament meeting. To my surprise, my parents attended. I was grateful for their moral support, as there were many new members in the ward I did not recognize. As people congratulated me on my successful mission, my parents beamed with pride. After the meeting, the missionaries asked to give them the discussions, but my father quickly declined. "No thank you," he said in his firm way that brooked no argument.

"Maybe some other time." My mother smiled at the elders to soften my father's terse reply. The missionaries smiled back and shrugged. They turned to talk to others nearby while my parents and I started for the chapel doors.

"Well, welcome home, Ariana," said a sweet, drawling voice behind me.

"Aimee?" I said in surprise, turning to exchange the customary kisses with the blonde girl who had once been on Jean-Marc's missionary team with me.

She lifted her head slightly, the better to show me her long, curly locks. "Do you like it?"

"Yes, it's very pretty." And it was. She had grown out her hair and had lightened it slightly so that with her expertly applied makeup, she looked like an American movie star. I felt suddenly dowdy, with my dark-brown hair cropped short and little makeup on my face.

"Are you coming to the baptisms?" she asked. I nodded, and she continued. "It will be the last time we can see Elder Perrault, since he's going home tomorrow." She smiled at me prettily, revealing her perfect white teeth. "Of course, I'm going to go visit him soon. I don't want him to forget me."

It took a while for me to realize that she was talking about my Jean-Marc. But, of course, no one knew about how close we'd become. I hadn't told anyone but my parents and Monique, and

Jean-Marc certainly wasn't discussing me with Aimee. I almost laughed.

"I'll see you there, Aimee," I said lightly. "I want to see Elder Perrault, too." She must have seen something she didn't like in my smile, because she frowned abruptly.

"Until later, then." She walked off, mincing as she went. My eyes followed her—as did those of every unattached man in the ward above the age of twelve.

Maybe it was because of Aimee that I took such great pains in getting myself ready that afternoon. But I didn't think so. I wanted to look good for Jean-Marc. I wore a new, close-fitting dress that was modest, but that made the best of my small waist and womanly curves. My thick hair was brushed to a shine, makeup applied carefully but not heavily. Afterward, I surveyed myself in the bathroom mirror and felt pleased with what I saw—eyes dancing with excitement, smooth, white skin flushed in anticipation, love beckoning in my expression.

"You look beautiful, Ariana." My mother glanced up from the couch as I came to say goodbye.

"Thanks," I said breathlessly. "But I'm a little nervous."

"Would you like us to go with you?" my father asked.

I smiled. At any other time, I would have jumped for joy that my parents were volunteering to go see the baptisms; but today I wanted to be alone. "No, thanks. I think this is something I want to do myself."

My mother returned my smile. "We understand. Good luck."

By the time I arrived, the church was already teeming with missionaries, members, investigators, and those to be baptized. People stood laughing and talking quietly in the halls and foyer. Almost immediately I saw Jean-Marc. He was near his companion and Aimee was with them, talking animatedly and fawning over Jean-Marc as much as she could without breaking the mission rules. He looked up and our eyes met. The intensity of his expression and my echoing feelings surprised even me. I could actually feel the magnetism between us. Suddenly, it was as if we were alone in the foyer, the many people disappearing as if by magic. No one else existed for either of us. It was all I could do not to run across the room and throw myself into his arms.

As if from a long distance away, I heard a pouting voice saying, "Are you listening to me, Elder Perrault?" I knew it was Aimee, and I also knew that Jean-Marc wasn't hearing a word she said. His eyes were still locked with mine, as were his emotions and thoughts.

"Jean-Marc!" I crossed the few feet between us in an instant.

"Ari!" he reached for my hand and grasped it tightly. "You're really here!"

"Of course I am! You think I'd give up a chance to see you before you left? Just wait until—"

"Excuse me." A loud male voice said, cutting me off. I turned to see Jean-Marc's American companion watching us. "Aren't you going to introduce me, Elder? Not that I can't tell who she is by all the photographs you have of her." He laughed, and to my delight, a slight blush crept over Jean-Marc's features.

"Sure. Elder, this is Ari—Ariana to you, however. I reserve Ari for myself. Ari, this is an elder, my companion, and that's all you have to know about him!"

The elder laughed. "He's afraid I'll charm you away from him. I'm Elder Madsen." The tall elder stuck out his hand, and Jean-Marc reluctantly let mine go so that I could shake with his companion. As I did so, I saw Aimee behind them, red with anger. She flipped her hair at me and stalked off. The others didn't notice her leaving.

The garrulous Elder Madsen was still talking. "Now, Elder Perrault here keeps telling me—and everyone else he meets—about you and showing a picture he keeps in a cardboard envelope in his notebook. He keeps telling us how many people you are baptizing, what a great example you are, and how much more beautiful you are than anyone else's girlfriend." He leaned toward me conspiratorially. "Now, of course, I didn't believe him until now. But he was right. And now I want to know one thing." He turned to Jean-Marc. "What makes you think you deserve this woman? I mean, besides being the top-baptizing elder in our mission, what else have you done to prove yourself to her?" We all laughed at that, and the conversation went on. But through it all I felt Jean-Marc's eyes on me, drinking in my presence as I was his. I felt happy and content.

Before long the baptisms were over, and it was time to go.

"Goodbye, Jean-Marc," I said softly. "But not for long."

I expected him to smile and tell me when he was going to call so we could begin carrying out the future we'd been planning for months in our letters. But instead, he frowned and looked at me seriously. "Ari, I need to do some thinking about things. I'll call or write you soon."

A chill swept through me, and I looked at him sharply. But he stared at me with such longing and love in his eyes that I dropped my suspicions immediately.

The next few weeks passed by, agonizingly slow and painful as I waited for Jean-Marc to call or write. Countless times I picked up the phone myself, only to put it down again. I knew it was my pride that was stopping me, but I wouldn't force myself on a man who didn't love me.

My depression deepened, and through it all I kept questioning myself. Had I imagined that he loved me? Imagined the look in his eyes? Was it only me who had fallen in love? I brought out the letters he had written during our missions, and there was no mistaking the words. He had loved me, had been planning a future with me, but something had happened. What? Try as I might, I couldn't find the answers.

Another side of me reasoned that Jean-Marc was busy at home after being away for two years. Even now, he was probably thinking up a creative way to propose. I remembered his engaging grin and the laughing, green-brown eyes so full of love, the way his voice had caressed my name, the long letters that had promised so much more.

What had happened?

"He's probably having problems adjusting after his mission," Monique said to me one Sunday at the end of November, exactly a month since I had seen Jean-Marc. We had arrived a little early for sacrament meeting and were talking quietly in the chapel. I enjoyed having Monique with me again. She and her husband were visiting our ward to show off their new baby, a little girl with light-brown hair and dark eyes. Envy of Monique and her life swept through me as I remembered what I had lost. But I forced the feelings down. Monique, too, had been through a great deal with the death of her parents before finding the Church and eventually a good, worthy man to take her to the temple. I didn't begrudge her that life; I just wanted it for myself.

"You know," she continued, "when my husband got off his mission he acted really strange at first, like he was in shock or something. Then suddenly he came around, and everything fell into place."

"Yes, but why wouldn't he at least write?" I glanced around the chapel with its beautiful organ music sounding softly through the room, cushioned wooden benches, many chandeliers, and the smiling congregation gathering. But it seemed that no matter where I looked, I saw Jean-Marc. "Paulette has even written once, but she didn't say a word about Jean-Marc, even though I asked her about him. Oh, why doesn't he call?"

"Well, did *you* write to *him?*" Monique asked quietly as she cuddled her baby close to her. Seeing her, I felt my arms ache with emptiness.

I shook my head. "He as much as told me not to that last day I saw him—to wait until he called me. I didn't understand how he could say that while looking at me like he did. I still don't."

Monique nodded in agreement. "He always did stare at you like that—his eyes filled with love and longing. After you left, he carried that picture I took of you everywhere. He even showed it to the mission president and told him you were the woman he was going to marry. I was there when he did it. The president shrugged and said that was wonderful, as long as he kept baptizing and didn't break the mission rules. From the president's pained expression, I gathered Jean-Marc had told him all about you many times before." She frowned sympathetically. "I'm sorry, Ariana. What he's doing now doesn't make any sense. I don't know what to tell you. I can't figure out why he hasn't called or written."

Just then, a sweetly malicious voice came from the bench behind us. Aimee. I stiffened immediately. How much of our conversation had she heard? Monique and I both turned our heads to see the blonde beauty sitting forward on the bench behind us, elbows coming to rest on the back of the bench we were sitting on.

"I thought I heard you mention Jean-Marc," she said with fake innocence. She flipped her long hair over her shoulder with a practiced hand and threw a teasing glance at a young man a few rows over who was staring at her. "Have you received a letter from him?"

I wanted to lie, or tell her it wasn't any of her business, but I couldn't find words. I didn't need to. She already knew I hadn't heard from Jean-Marc, if not by my desolate expression then by her eavesdropping. I simply shook my head.

"Well, I received a letter from him only this week, and I've talked to him many times on the phone." Her beautiful greenish eyes glittered, but beneath the beauty I saw the hardness of her white face. "I'll be going to see him soon."

I stared at her, not wanting to believe my ears, though I could hear the truth in her voice. She actually *had* received a letter from Jean-Marc.

I didn't cry or hit her smug face as I wanted to, but carefully masked my feelings. There was no way I would let her see how deeply her words cut into my heart. I had had much practice with pain, and I could hide it well.

But I couldn't help the thoughts of Jacques that came fleetingly to my mind, and how terribly he had let me down. *Were all men that way?* I asked myself bitterly. *Even those who are members of the true church?*

Now Aimee turned to Monique and began to gush over the baby. "What a beautiful baby, Monique! She looks just like you. I can't wait until my future husband," she shot a meaningful glance at me, "and I have one. May I please hold her?"

"I'm sorry," Monique said pleasantly enough. But I, who knew her well, could feel the chill in her voice. "I promised Ariana that she could hold her next." As she spoke, she was handing me the baby.

Aimee frowned. "Another time, then. The meeting will begin soon, and I've just got to talk to Henri over there before it starts." She motioned with a careless hand to the young man who had been staring at her. "Goodbye now." She stood and walked away, leaving us in a cloud of her expensive perfume.

"Don't mind her," Monique whispered. "There's no way Jean-Marc could love a girl like Aimee. She's not real. He'd see right through her."

I had thought so too—until now.

"She's not really that bad," Monique continued. "She just has a lot of growing up to do."

I nodded, but was relieved when Bishop Rameau stood at the podium to start the meeting. Now Monique would not expect a reply. I felt my heart break, threatening to plunge me into the abyss of gloom and despair I had felt after Nette's death, when I had believed myself all alone.

The only thing that saved me was the precious gift from heaven cuddled in my arms. Monique's baby. I buried my face into her fuzzy hair, breathing in all the baby smells of her, holding her to my chest, feeling her trusting innocence. She opened her eyes to look at me. Those dark eyes, so wise, still filled with heaven's glory. Eyes that reminded me of Nette's.

I felt the pressure of Monique's hand against my leg. I looked over to see tears in her eyes. "You hold her for as long as you need," she whispered. I smiled and nodded. But after a time I gave the infant back to her mother. She was rooting around to nurse, and I had no milk to give her.

CHAPTER SIXTEEN

Aimee caught me at church a week later. This time Monique was not there to buffer her attack. It had been raining steadily all morning—wet, cold, and depressing. I had participated in the church meetings, had drunk them in like a man stranded in the desert drinks the clear waters of his rescuers. But now I had to go out into the dismal, cold day.

I stood staring out the double glass doors before I left the church building, trying to sort out my future. I was planning to go back to school in January, and had already moved up a position at the bank. In fact, I was fast becoming my father's right hand. I loved the work and adored being with my father, but I missed Jean-Marc endlessly. I still hadn't given up hope of working out whatever it was that had come between us.

But what?

Aimee?

I thought not, but men were sometimes hard to decipher.

"Oh, it's raining," said Aimee's sweet soprano voice behind me, interrupting my thoughts. "Now I'll have to ask one of the men for a ride home." Her voice didn't sound too disappointed. She studied me closely, beautiful as always in her modern dress, hair arranged just so, makeup accentuating her green eyes and thin face. "Have you heard from Jean-Marc?" she asked suddenly, her voice almost too casual.

I sighed. "Oh, Aimee. What does it matter to you?"

Her chin raised slightly, her eyes held mine. "Because I love him.

Oh, I know that you were close, and that he wrote you while you were on your mission. We couldn't write, you know, since I lived in his mission, but I saw him a great deal. I often went to see him on Sundays, even when he wasn't nearby. He was always glad to see me. We are good friends, and now that he has finished his mission, I intend to make him see me as much more than a friend."

"What makes you think he wants you as more than a friend?" I asked abruptly. I wasn't trying to be rude; I really wanted to know.

She pulled back as if I had slapped her. "He at least has written *me,*" she hissed spitefully. "He still hasn't written you, has he, Ariana? I thought not. You see, it's one thing to be friends and to write letters, but when it comes down to choosing a wife, a man has to consider a woman's past. A man has to be sure that such temptations as drugs, immorality, and such won't get in the way of an eternal relationship." She looked at me pointedly. "And we both know your past is none too good, Ariana. Maybe you're not worthy of a man like Jean-Marc."

I would have slapped her for real then, but she whirled away before I could do anything. And I would have sent words as evil and hateful as her own ripping into her back, but she had already disappeared into a room down the hall. Instead, I shook my head in amazement. How could she talk about eternity and my past in the same sentence? My life before I knew the Church was gone, forgiven, and forgotten, or so I had thought. Evidently some people did not forget easily.

I left the church, whose steeple rose high and beckoning into the low, dark clouds. Not bothering to pull my hood over my head, I made my way to the metro, hoping the freezing, snow-like rain would hide my tears and wishing I had accepted my father's offer to use his car. Unpleasant and dangerous as driving in Paris sometimes can be, at least I wouldn't have had time to think about the words Aimee had said—words that were eating away at me as I walked.

Those words never left me that week as I struggled to work and to forge a new life without my dreams of Jean-Marc. I was failing miserably, because deep down inside I knew Aimee was right. Why would a man choose a woman with a past when he could choose one who had always been in the Church? No, not Aimee; I could never believe that Jean-Marc would choose a woman like her. But maybe there was someone else. Perhaps a woman like Monique, who had never broken the law of chastity or stooped to drinking and drugs. Was that why Jean-Marc hadn't written? Was he worried about my future faithfulness? Had he turned to someone else because of this fear?

The more I thought about it, the more likely I thought it to be true. *Should I call him and tell him not to worry?*

I was at work when I had the idea to call him, but even as I thought to do so, I began doubting myself. Was I really on the straight and narrow? Could I be truly free from that old life forever? What if I wasn't worthy of Jean-Marc? I loved him so much and wanted him to succeed in life, and especially in the Church. What if I wasn't the woman who could help him reach his eternal goals? Suddenly the ache in my head matched the one in my heart. I put my head in my hands and closed my eyes.

"Why don't you knock off early today, Ari?" my father said. I looked up from my desk at the bank to see him standing anxiously over me. "You've put in enough time as it is this week, and you deserve a couple of hours off today."

I shook my head and stared down at the papers I was going through. But I couldn't focus on them. I sighed. "Maybe you're right, Father. Besides, I can always take these with me."

He smiled. "Sometimes I think you're too much like me."

I stood up to hug him. "I like that idea."

"It's going to be all right," he said, tightening his arms around me. "I know you're going through a tough time right now, but you'll find your way. And your mother and I are here for you—this time." The last two words were said with regret, and I knew he was thinking of Antoine.

I would have gone home, but as I was leaving, someone stopped me just inside the bank.

"Hey, Ariana!"

I looked over to see a man my age coming from one of the tellers. He had long brown hair that hung like strings around him. His face, which seemed crowlike with his hooked nose and thin, darting features, was darkened with beard stubble, and an unlit cigarette dangled from his lips. He was wearing old jeans which were ripped at the knees, dirty tennis shoes, a faded green sweater, and a worn jacket.

I didn't know who he was.

"It's me—Maurice," he said, seeing my blank expression. "One of your old gang. Jacques' friend . . ." His voice trailed off as he waited for me to remember, to look past the years and lifestyles that separated us.

"Oh, yeah, I remember. It's been a long time." We were walking out the door now.

"Hey, come have a drink with me for old times," he urged, holding up a white envelope. "My parents sent me some money for Christmas, so I'm good for it." He smiled, revealing yellowing teeth. I was revolted at the sight, but he looked at me so hopefully. "Please," he said as I hesitated. "There isn't anyone left from the old gang anymore. We all went our own ways. Can't you spare a few minutes to talk about old times? Remember, it's Christmas. You know, goodwill and peace on earth and all that."

Christmas was still over two weeks away, but I nodded. "Okay. But only one drink, and nothing alcoholic. And I choose the place."

His expression was puzzled, but he shrugged his agreement. We walked together down the street and to the next, finally finding a cafe with a bar that didn't look too sleazy. I went in and Maurice followed. He immediately ordered two beers, but I asked for hot chocolate. "I forgot about the no alcohol," he said sheepishly.

I took off my coat and laid it on my lap over my thin briefcase. "That's okay. So what have you been doing these past years?" As I asked the question, the bartender brought the two beers and hot chocolate.

"Nothing much. Just hanging out, working from time to time. I get kind of lonely for the good old days. I sometimes go see Jacques at the prison, but he's different now. Ever gone there?"

I shook my head. "No reason to. You knew we're divorced, didn't you?"

"Yeah, but you never know."

"I have seen Paulette, though." I told him how she was living in Bordeaux and planning to be married in February. We also talked a lot about our shared past. The memories hurt more than I cared to admit.

The small bar was rapidly filling with people, mostly men coming from work. The wild crowd, the kind I had always run with, usually didn't come in until later. I remembered how out of place I had felt at first, but how they had accepted me and loved me when I hadn't anyone else. I also remembered how the drinking had dimmed the pain of Antoine's loss; even now I could feel the taste of it on my lips, the warmth spreading through the cold in my heart. Oh, how I could use that warmth now! Temptation struck hard and quick, and feeling as hopeless as I did about my own future and self-worth, it was almost too much to bear.

"I always liked you, Ariana," Maurice said suddenly. "I would have tried for you if Jacques hadn't come along." He watched me for a minute before continuing. "You look pretty depressed now. Tell me, what's wrong? Or wait, I have something better." He reached into his coat pocket and withdrew a thin, homemade cigarette that I knew was full of marijuana. He thrust it into my hand, and I sat clutching it in surprise.

I was embarrassed to be holding it, but worse was the fact that at that moment I would have given almost anything to smoke it, for it would temporarily make me forget that I wasn't worthy enough for Jean-Marc, or any other good man in the Church. And what was my future worth without Jean-Marc, whom I loved more than I could express? Better to drown myself in alcohol and drugs than to risk disappointment time and time again.

But something inside me rebelled at that, and at the last instant before giving in, I remembered to pray to the One who had never let me down. *Oh, Father, please help me out of this!* I begged silently. *I don't know what I'm doing, and I'm so afraid!* And at that precise moment my salvation came, though certainly not in the form I would have chosen.

Aimee.

I glanced up to see her watching me in the doorway, triumph etched on her face. The homemade cigarette slipped through my fingers and instantly I was saved, freed from the almost magical hold it had over me. What on earth was I thinking? Could I forget my daughter and how she died? I knew better than this! Suddenly everything was clear, and I found myself again.

Maurice chose that second to lean over and kiss me, clumsily but passionately, his arms reaching around me in a tight embrace. As if in slow motion, I saw Aimee's green eyes grow even wider, her triumph more pronounced. I pushed Maurice forcefully away. "I'll be right back," I muttered, slipping off the bar stool to confront Aimee, who had turned to leave.

"Aimee! Wait!"

She was already outside in the cold December afternoon before she turned to face me, a mocking smile on her pretty lips.

"So, Ariana," she began before I could explain. "I see you have fallen back into your old ways. Jean-Marc will be sad to hear that his precious Ari has been drinking and smoking, and even has a new boyfriend."

"It isn't what it seems," I protested. But I knew she wasn't going to listen.

"Isn't it? There you are in a bar, with a beer in front of you and a cigarette in your hand, kissing a man who's obviously a drug addict. Those things add up, Ariana, to one thing. Don't the scriptures say something about a dog turning back to his vomit? Well, that's what you're doing, and I'm glad Jean-Marc has thought to reconsider his involvement with you. What kind of wife could you possibly make him?"

I could feel my face burning as my anger grew. All at once it exploded. "You hypocrite! You talk about my past as if it's something you personally have to forgive, as if you're the judge of my worthiness! Oh, yes, you even had *me* wondering. But not anymore. I suddenly see everything clearly. I know my Savior loves me, and that he died for my sins! They are gone, every one of them. And if you don't believe it, then you have a lot of searching to do, because that means you don't believe in the atonement of Jesus Christ, that he can really do what he promised: take away our sins so we can be free of them forever. Well, I see the truth now. When I looked up to see you there, so ready to judge me, I suddenly realized that you haven't the right! No one on earth has! And as for Jean-Marc, if he does feel the way you claim, if he can't forget my past, then *he's* not worthy of *me!*

No husband of mine will ever doubt the power of Jesus Christ!"

I left her and went back into the bar, letting her spiteful retort disappear into the air: "I'll tell Jean-Marc about you. I promise I will!"

But it made no difference to me. I was free of her, and what she thought no longer mattered. The change in me wasn't complete; but I had seen the situation as it truly was, and now I needed time to sort it all out. But first I had to face Maurice.

"Maurice, I don't feel romantically about you," I said firmly. "In fact, I'm in love with someone else, though I don't know how things are going to work out between us. Besides, my life is different now. You and I don't live in the same world." Then my missionary spirit kicked in. "But I would like to introduce you to my world, if you're willing. It's not an easy way, but it's much better. Paulette found it, too." He just stared at me, and I knew he didn't know what to say. I hastily pulled my extra Book of Mormon out of my briefcase. I opened it to write my phone number below the missionaries' number I had already printed there, along with my testimony. As I did so, my sheet of ten names fell out. I looked at it for a moment, then put it back into my briefcase.

"Here, consider this your Christmas gift." I handed him the book. "If you are curious, call the first number. They are missionaries and can tell you all about it. The other number is mine. Call whenever you want to talk. Leave a message when I'm not home, and I'll call you back. Or come to the bank. Will you do that?"

"Yeah, sure, Ariana." His eyes went curiously to the book; but I had been a missionary long enough to know that if you left it up to the investigator, sometimes things never got off the ground. "What about your number, do you have one?" Maurice nodded, and I wrote it in my address book. I slipped it back inside my briefcase and shut it with a decisive snap. "I have to go now. I've got a lot to do."

He nodded, and I touched his shoulder briefly. "It was nice seeing you." I turned and left, walking purposely though I didn't have any destination immediately in mind. I knew only that I had to sort out what had happened, to understand it completely. My feet traced the familiar path to the Seine River, and I walked along it as I used to with Antoine and then with Nette. It had been a long time since I had come, maybe too long. The wind was blowing slightly and the cold air hurt my lungs. I pushed my scarf up to cover my mouth so that my thoughts could race unhampered by the searing in my throat.

Jesus died for me! He paid for what I did in the past! How could I have lost sight of that? I thought of Paulette and how she had been so afraid that her sins were too deep and too many to ever be forgiven, and how I had assured her that the Atonement was expansive and profound enough to cover anything, if we were willing. Jesus, a God, had done the suffering, and he would remember our sins no more. The familiar and beloved scripture played across my mind: "Though your sins be as scarlet, they shall be as white as snow; though they be red like crimson, they shall be as wool."

I thought about Aimee, too, and I suddenly saw that she was hurting. She may be right about Jean-Marc worrying that I might not be worthy, but she knew he didn't want her, either. In the words "his precious Ari," she had revealed to me that there was more to her story than she wanted me to know. But it really made no difference. If Jean-Marc loved me, he would have contacted me. What Aimee said or did shouldn't make any difference.

Sorrow nearly overcame me at the thought of Jean-Marc, his gaze so intense and caressing, the words of love in his many letters. I loved him so much—more than I had ever dreamed of loving even Jacques, the man I had once married.

I stopped walking now, and set my briefcase down on the short stone wall that looked down over the Seine. I stood leaning there with my hands pressed against the rock, feeling them slowly numbing from the cold and wishing the feeling could extend to my heart, at least to the part that ached for Jean-Marc. Boats passed in the river below, some cargo, a few with passengers, leaving paths of rough water in their wake, unmindful of their solitary observer and the tumultuous feelings within my soul.

Oh, Jean-Marc! How can I go on without you?

But at the same time, a thought came so firmly into my mind that it seemed as if I was hearing it with my earthly ears instead of my spirit: "Trust in Me." Hope filled my heart. Yes, that is what I would do. I would have faith in the Lord and believe that he would do what was best for me. I would believe that even if things didn't work out the way I had wanted, they would work out somehow, and I would be happy. I clung to this thought as a drowning man clings to a piece of flotsam wood. For eighteen months I had taught others about faith and repentance; but only now had I truly begun to understand how they applied to *my* life.

"I will make it!" I said aloud and triumphantly. The cold breeze lifted my words out across the river like a promise.

I still loved Jean-Marc, still yearned for him, but I knew that I could—and would—survive without him. The thought, though aching and raw, came as a welcome relief. Within myself I had discovered the power to be happy, with or without Jean-Marc. My thoughts once again turned to the Savior and the plan of redemption. I realized that once and for all, I had finally and completely forgiven myself for Nette's death, as I had Paulette. There was only one more thing I had to do.

With numb hands, I opened my briefcase and retrieved the list of names I had given Jean-Marc so long ago. The cold air began to blow more forcefully in my face, but I didn't stop, not even when my scarf fell back and let the searing wind into my nose and throat. Filled with purpose, I unfolded the paper and reached for a pen. Firmly, I wrote in the last name.

Jacques de Cotte.

I remembered what I had told Elisabeth that day when she learned that Paulette had been with Jacques when he had given Nette the drugs—how we would be forgiven by the same spirit we forgave. The scripture I had been referring to was in Luke 6:37: "Judge not, and ye shall not be judged; condemn not, and ye shall not be condemned; forgive, and ye shall be forgiven."

Once, I had believed that God would punish Jacques for killing Nette. It never occurred to me that he wouldn't go to hell and burn forever; indeed, the thought had given me comfort in those first lonely months without my daughter. That he might repent and be forgiven didn't even cross the far reaches of my consciousness. But, after all, he hadn't murdered our baby in cold blood; it had been a horrible, drug-induced nightmare, and just maybe he was ready to go on with his life.

And I knew I had to forgive him.

I didn't have to love him or visit him daily, but I had to start him on the path back, to free him from my anger and accusations. After feeling Aimee's scorn and seeing how desperately Paulette had yearned for my forgiveness, I knew I had to at least give him that. The thought frightened me, and my heart beat rapidly and painfully. *How could I face him again?*

Chapter Seventeen

I t took me over two weeks to get up the courage to go see Jacques at the prison. I wanted to make sure that I really had forgiven him deep down. It was much more difficult than it had been to forgive Paulette, because he had betrayed my love, all my hopes, and my trust. I finally decided there was only one way I would know for sure: to see him face to face.

I went on Christmas morning. My parents were sleeping in after the eating and present-opening we had done at midnight, and I didn't tell them I was going. This was something I had to do alone.

The morning was very clear and cold, but windless. I was dressed in thick black stretch pants and a dark-brown ribbed shirt. I had chosen the outfit carefully; it was sober but flattering to my coloring and features. I had always looked good in dark colors. I didn't know why I wanted to look good, but I spent extra time that morning getting ready for my visit. At least the confidence my appearance gave me helped calm the pounding of my heart.

There was almost no one out on the streets yet, and I walked toward the metro calmly, moving briskly to keep myself warm. My heavy, thigh-length coat was more than adequate, but I felt a chill of terror spreading out from my heart in anticipation of what I was about to do. The public transport was operating even on Christmas, and as I settled into my seat in the metro, I felt grateful that I would not have to drive. My hands were shaking badly, and it was not only from the cold.

The rhythm of the underground train soon had me relaxing, and my mind recalled the previous Sunday when I had born my testimony. It hadn't been fast Sunday, but a few days earlier I had been called in to talk with the bishop, who had asked me to be the new Young Women's president. I accepted with trepidation. During our conversation, I told him about Jean-Marc, about Aimee and the incident at the cafe, and also about my plans to go see Jacques. There were tears in both of our eyes when I finished.

"I wish everyone could understand the Atonement as you are learning to," Bishop Rameau said quietly. "I think too many times we are hard on ourselves and too quick to judge others in an attempt to ease our own feelings of inferiority." He paused. "Do you feel able to tell your story to our members? I feel it could greatly help them."

Hesitantly, I agreed.

The next few days I had prayed about what I would say, and about choosing my counselors. Strangely, a particular name kept coming to mind. On Saturday, I gave Bishop Rameau my names written on a piece of paper, and he smiled when he saw them.

"I'll ask them tomorrow," he said almost laughingly. "These are just the people I would have chosen myself. But I want you to talk in church before I ask them. I know it's unusual to call a president without counselors, but I want them to hear your testimony first."

Sunday dawned bright and cold. I went to church, once more accompanied by my parents. When the bishop read my name to sustain me, I looked at Aimee. She stared at me, and I almost expected her hand to be raised in opposition. But she didn't raise her hand at all, not even to sustain.

"Now," the bishop continued, "I'd like our new Young Women's president to speak to us."

I smiled nervously at the bishop as I approached the podium. The congregation seemed much larger from up in front, and I swallowed once or twice before beginning. I was used to talking and teaching others, but today was different; I no longer had the mantle of a missionary to sustain me. My parents were smiling up at me encouragingly, and Aimee's green eyes fixed on my face. The others around them blurred, and I felt that my talk was only for these three.

The words came slowly, then more quickly as I told of my

feelings of self-doubt, the experience in the cafe, and my ensuing understanding of forgiveness. I told them about Paulette and Jacques, but I didn't once mention Aimee or Jean-Marc. My testimony rang out strong and true, and I saw many with tears in their eyes. Finally, I was finished and sat down, my eyes once again searching for Aimee's. She was crying and looking at me sorrowfully.

Afterward, she came up and hugged me. "I'm so sorry. I didn't realize what I was doing. I was blind, I think. Please forgive me."

"Does that mean you'll serve as Ariana's first counselor?" Bishop Rameau asked, suddenly appearing at my elbow.

Aimee's eye widened in shock. She turned an incredulous face to me. "Me? You want *me?* Why?"

"I don't know, I just do." I hugged her and we both made fools of ourselves, weeping like babies.

"I—there's so much I want to tell you about Jean-Marc," she whispered in my ear. "I was just so hurt that—"

"It doesn't matter, Aimee," I cut her short. "Neither of us needs Jean-Marc to live. We will become the best we can be. And we will be happy."

She nodded, her golden locks bouncing. "But I still want to tell you."

I sighed, suddenly feeling the weight of the extreme emotions I'd been through that day. "Later. In a few weeks, when things calm down. Not today."

Aimee agreed, and I hadn't seen her since except at a planning meeting at my house where we hadn't been alone to talk. My other counselor, secretary, and my mother had also been present, coming up with ideas for the Young Women. Until now, I had even forgotten Aimee's comment in the face of my new responsibilities.

The day of our meeting, my mother had also been excited, and had pitched in many good ideas. Not for the first time, I found myself thinking that she would make an excellent member.

My thoughts came slowly back to the present, and I found I had almost reached my destination. I got up and walked carefully to the doors, remembering how Antoine had hung on the bars that last night in the stopped train. I smiled. This time there was no pain.

The train slowed, and the doors slid open to let me out. I still had a good walk in front of me to reach the prison, but I didn't mind. I had called several days before to ask about the visiting hours and procedures, and now my watch told me I had plenty of time.

When I reached the prison, I was immediately ushered to a desk where I had to show identification and sign some papers. Then I went through a metal detector and into a hall, led by a strong-looking guard who whistled Christmas tunes. One side of the corridor was made of glass; I could see the inmates inside, sitting at long tables with various friends and family members. Some seemed happy, some sad and sullen. *I guess we choose our attitudes no matter where we are,* I thought.

I saw Jacques before he saw me, and I stopped a moment at the glass to study him. He was waiting at one end of a table. At the other end, a fellow inmate was deep in conversation with two friends who had come to spread Christmas cheer. Jacques was watching them a little wistfully, his dark-blond head tilted to one side. His hair was cropped shorter than I'd ever seen it; other than that he hadn't changed much physically, except that maybe he was a little thinner. He was dressed in prison blue like all the other inmates.

Memories of the past shook me and I wanted to flee, to run back the way I had come and be free of Jacques forever. But deep inside, I knew this was the only way we could both be free. I had loved him once, had had a child with him, and despite the anguish raging through my heart, I would do this.

I watched him a minute more and then shook myself. I wasn't doing any good here, peering through the window like a child spying. I resumed walking, quickening my pace to reach the guard who was waiting at the entrance to the visiting room. He smiled gently, which surprised me, but all at once I felt the fear on my face as well as the pain. Glancing at the glass window beside the door, I saw my white face, just for an instant, stark and stiff against large eyes and brown hair, alabaster framed in dark shadow. My lower lip was trembling, and I bit it to still the movement. I swallowed once, closing my eyes briefly to find courage, prayed, and then walked into the room.

He looked up as I entered, sad brown eyes fixed on me, never flickering for an instant, a tentative smile on his face.

I sat across the table from him. "Hi, Jacques."

"Hi, Ariana," he replied warily. "I never thought I'd see you again."

I returned his steady gaze. "Nor I you."

"You look really good," he ventured. "You've cut your hair short, like when we first met."

I didn't reply, but sat there staring at him. The old attraction I had for Jacques was completely gone. Instead of the wild, desperate urge for him to love me, I felt only sadness and acceptance.

"Why are you here?" he asked with trepidation. His hands clutched the edge of the table as he steeled himself for my response. I knew he was afraid of what I might say. In his eyes there was also a glimmer of hope, which he quickly squelched before it began to mean too much.

I glanced away for an instant, trying to find a way to begin. At the other end of the table the inmate was telling a story to his two visitors, arms raised in animation as he spoke. On one thick arm he had a tattoo of an anchor. I was feeling lost and scared, but the anchor seemed to strengthen me, to remind me that my anchor was my God, and that with him nothing was impossible.

"Ariana." Jacques' voice was agonized. "I never did drugs again after that night. It's been three years now. It wasn't because I was in here, either; those who want them know how to get drugs, even here. But I didn't want to ever forget what I did that night. I will never forgive myself—ever—for what happened to our baby." His voice was dead, and I abruptly tore my gaze away from the tattoo anchor to see the terrible mask of suffering that was Jacques' face. His eyes were completely devoid of hope.

My eyes flashed again to the anchor, then back to Jacques' face. "But I forgive you," I said softly.

The incredulous, wondrous look on his face made me glad I had come. Under my very gaze, he became more alive. And as I watched that change take place in him, somehow I, too, was freed from the chains that had bound my spirit to the past.

"But why? How?" he asked. His hands were still gripping the table so tightly that the fingers were dead white against the dark hairs, the blood vessels standing out grotesquely.

I gave him my best missionary smile. "That's a long story."

"Well, I've got time," he said seriously.

I began from the first time I had seen the missionaries to the present, leaving nothing out, not even my feelings for Jean-Marc. At times Jacques' eyes showed disbelief, yet at others I knew he understood and accepted. We talked the entire allotted time at the prison. When it was time to go, I handed him a blue book.

"The Book of Mormon," Jacques read the cover aloud. He opened it to see my testimony and the missionaries' number, pamphlets, a list of reading assignments, and one thing more: a picture of his daughter.

He started to cry, taking in loud, heaving breaths, and I thought my heart would break all over again for him. "Thank you," he whispered when he had recovered slightly. "Thank you so much."

"Will you see my friends the missionaries, Jacques?" I asked him fervently. "Will you at least let them explain? Maybe then you can make sense of all this and forgive yourself."

He nodded. "Yes, Ariana. For you I will."

I stood up to leave, but he reached out a hand to stop me. "Jean-Marc would be a fool not to see what he has in you." He glanced down at the ground and added, "As I was." After a brief moment he looked up at me again earnestly. "You are a true lady, Ariana. A queen like you always talked about. And you'll get the best, because that's what you deserve. I only wish I hadn't hurt you so much."

I smiled and shrugged. "I know. I also wish it had never happened. But, Jacques, the making of a queen or a king is never easy, you know, though terribly worth it in the end." We stood looking at each other without speaking, sharing a bond that could only be felt by those who had faced joint tragedy and survived.

Then I said softly, "Goodbye, Jacques. I hope you have a good life. I hope you can be happy."

"You too, Ariana. And thanks for coming."

"You're welcome, Jacques." I left without a backward glance, feeling lighter and happier than I had since Jean-Marc had deserted me. What was it Jacques had said? Oh, yes, that Jean-Marc would be a fool not to see what he had in me.

That was strange; Jean-Marc had never struck me as a fool.

Chapter Eighteen

After leaving the prison, I went straight home. The afternoon was very cold and an icy breeze had started blowing, yet inside my heart was warm. I was filled with a strange kind of contentment I had never felt before. I realized that these past few weeks I had learned to have faith in the Lord and accept his will, knowing it would be the best thing for me. I no longer needed others to make me happy, but could rely on my inner self that was buoyed by the constant power of my Savior. At last, I understood what it meant to have a testimony.

A part of me still ached for Jean-Marc and the love I had so hoped for, but I knew that time and the gospel would heal my wounds as they had the last time—wounds far deeper than I had now.

I was so intent on my inner thoughts that I was upon the man before I realized who he was. Suddenly, there was Jean-Marc, sitting on the cement steps outside my parents' apartment building! I had no time to prepare my reactions or steel myself to pretend that I didn't care. I felt my face light up with the love I had for him, though I could feel the hurt there as well.

"Jean-Marc, I—I didn't expect you," I stuttered as he jumped up to greet me. His face was reddened by the cold and his hair tousled by the light breeze. His expression was anxious as his green-brown eyes searched mine. I suddenly wished desperately for night to fall, to quickly hide my face, but the afternoon sun shone clearly and did nothing to mask my feelings. "Why have you come?" Tears gathered in my eyes.

"It's Christmas, Ari," he said in a hoarse, emotion-filled voice, blinking his eyes rapidly as if trying to stop his own tears. "I *had* to come."

"Why?" I really wanted to know. It had been almost two months since I had seen him at the baptisms, and I had been sure it was over between us.

Until now.

Jean-Marc stared miserably at me, his eyes filling with tears. "Why? Because I love you, Ari!" he declared passionately. I could feel the warmth of his breath against my face, and it was too much to bear. I dropped my gaze to the ground as he continued. "I have always loved you, since the very first day I met you. It wasn't just the way you looked, it was the way your soul touched mine, the way you threw yourself into the gospel so wholeheartedly after going through the worst nightmare any woman could imagine! It was the way you made up with your parents and helped Paulette, even though she was partly responsible for Nette's death." He paused and gave a short, mirthless laugh. "I wouldn't be surprised if you had already forgiven Jacques and invited the missionaries to visit him!" He stopped talking as a sob shook him. I was still staring at the ground, unable to believe what I was hearing. After all, there was still the matter of those two months between us. Why had he left me so long without so much as a letter? He had hurt me so deeply—broken all my dreams. How could I trust him again?

But I knew I had to at least hear him out. I needed to understand why he had acted as he did so I could begin to heal properly, putting it behind me. Besides, I had learned that to be kind was important, even when—no, *especially* when it hurt.

"Oh, Ari!" Jean-Marc's voice was anguished, and he fell to his knees on the cobblestone sidewalk before me so he could look up into my downcast eyes. "I'm so sorry I haven't called you! You see, when you got off your mission and came to the church that day, you were so beautiful and confident, a true queen, worthy of all the blessings of the eternities—and I felt unworthy of you!" Now it was his turn to look down at the ground while I gazed upon him in amazement. The torment of self-doubt that I had also felt came back to me vividly, self-inflicted, but powerful and wrenching. I understood exactly what Jean-Marc was saying.

He paused a moment, as if organizing his thoughts, and then stared up into my teary eyes with a love so unmistakable that I wondered how I had ever doubted him. "If you remember, it was my companion who posed the question that day," he continued. "What made me think I deserved you? And I knew deep down that he was right. I kept staring at you, unable to get his words out of my mind. You had been through so much, refined way beyond me by fires I could not begin to imagine! You made it, despite where you came from, despite the horrible death of the daughter you loved more than life! You came up fighting, long after others would have given up, and I felt I had nothing to offer you! I have been a member almost all my life—I never even knew what it was to have a testimony until I went on my mission. I've never had to fight for anything or prove that I would stay true to the Lord no matter what.

"And there you were, a potential queen, and I suddenly knew that only a king could help you become a true queen one day. And, Ari . . ." His voice broke. "Ari, I didn't know if I could be a king, but I knew you deserved one. I loved you so much that there was no way I was going to hold you back."

Tears streamed down both our faces now, and I sank to the sidewalk with him, pulling him back to sit on the cement steps that led to my building, pressing my cheek hard against his so that our tears flowed together. A few passersby who had braved the cold Christmas weather watched us curiously, but we paid them no heed, being so caught up in our emotions.

I tried to speak, but Jean-Marc put a finger over my lips and continued. "So that's what I've been doing these past two months. I've been trying to see if I had the potential within me, no matter how deeply hidden, to become your eternal partner. I wanted to know that you and our children could rely on me, as I knew I could rely on you." His face looked pained as he remembered. "I was so afraid I would come up short. I studied, I prayed, talked to my bishop and my mother, prayed some more. And, Ari, I think that with your help, I can make myself the man you deserve—the man who will never let you down, and who will love the Lord as much as you do!"

"Oh, Jean-Marc," I whispered, so afraid, but knowing I was going to give him another chance, knowing I still loved him. "I could have told you that!"

He smiled a little sheepishly through his tears. "I realize that now. You see, only yesterday my little sister, Lu-Lu, brought it to my attention that I should give you more credit for picking a potential husband. She said that you probably knew me better than I knew myself, and that I was a dummy not to have told you how I was feeling right after my mission!"

"She was right."

Jean-Marc laughed and looked into my eyes, wiping away my tears with his fingers. "I promise never to try to solve the important things myself ever again, Ari. We'll do it together—as long as you promise to be my queen!"

"I will, Jean-Marc! I will!" I said exultantly, lifting my lips to his. After he kissed me I added, "But let's keep this queen thing to ourselves, okay? You know how we French feel about royalty . . . remember what they did to our last queen, Marie-Antoinette." I made a neck-chopping motion to emphasize my point. We laughed helplessly until the cold from the cement seeped into our bones, making us so stiff we could hardly move.

"Come, let's go inside and tell my parents," I urged, getting to my feet and pulling him with me.

He kissed me once more on the lips, passionate yet tender, full of promise. "Okay, Ari. I love you!" He paused and added teasingly, "But remember, I'll not have you smoking in front of our children!"

"What?" I exclaimed, trying to figure out what he was talking about. Then I had it. "Aimee—she *did* write to you! I hope you didn't—"

"Of course I didn't believe her! I realized there was probably more to the situation than she knew or was telling. I knew that whatever had happened that day, you came out on top! I figured she was just mad because I had written her to say I didn't feel romantically about her. You see, she had called and written me repeatedly, asking to come down to visit, alluding to our future together. I had to tell her that she and I had no future. She was the last thing I needed right then!"

"She's very beautiful," I said, just to see what he would say.

He shook his head. "No, she's very pretty, but never beautiful. *You're* beautiful, Ari!" He still had one arm around me, and with his free hand he stroked my hair. "I love your hair, so soft and cut short so I can see the curve of your neck, and those dark eyes that see into my soul. You are very beautiful! But there's more—the inside beauty that's even more important, your heavenly aura. You're everything to me, Ari!"

"I was tempted that day Aimee saw me," I admitted suddenly. I wanted only truth between us.

Jean-Marc smiled. "But once more you proved yourself, Ari, and it's over and done with. Now come, are we going to announce our engagement to your parents or not? I rang a few hours ago, but didn't go up since you weren't there. Now I'm so cold from waiting here that your parents will probably think I'm shaking in fear of them."

"You're not afraid of anything, Jean-Marc!" I turned to open the door with my key.

"That's not true," he said suddenly, his voice full of emotion. "I was so afraid you'd tell me no."

I left the key in the lock and threw my arms around him. "Make no mistake about it, Jean-Marc . . . I love you, and I'm going to marry you!"

CHAPTER NINETEEN

That Christmas was the best I'd had for some time. The weather was freezing, and we even saw a few flakes of snow in Paris; but Jean-Marc and I were warmed and comforted by the new light of our love. He didn't return to Bordeaux, except to get his things, and I went with him to do that. He stayed temporarily with Marguerite and Jules until we could find an apartment. We were determined to not be too far separated ever again.

In January, Jean-Marc began to work at my father's bank and to attend college, studying—of all things—accounting, for he shared my fascination with numbers. I, too, was taking classes, though we didn't share any since I was three semesters ahead of him. We rented a small apartment near my parents where he stayed, a place we would soon share. My bed and couch looked very good in the stylish apartment, and weekly we added new items to make it more comfortable. My mother especially went wild, buying things until, laughingly, we had to beg her to stop.

Paulette and Pierre were married civilly in February. They had chosen not to wait for Paulette to be a member one year before marrying. Considering their ages and their growing closeness, it was the best decision for them. We drove with my parents to Bordeaux to attend the wedding. My parents, who had gone principally to meet Jean-Marc's family, were amazed at the change in Paulette.

Paulette herself seemed more amazed than anyone. "I can't believe that I'm actually marrying Pierre!" she whispered to me just before the ceremony. We were in one of the classrooms in the church, standing before a huge mirror that Elisabeth, now large with her pregnancy, had set up for the bride.

I stared at Paulette in wonder. She had changed so much since that day I had found her sprawled on the sidewalk. Her light-brown eyes were clear of drugs and shining with love. Her rich brown hair now gleamed lustrously and was arranged in artful waves. Her hands, once dirty with broken nails, were now clean and strong, the nails cut short and even. Her skin was clear, and the pain and sadness that had aged her were gone. But the biggest change was in her spirit; the confidence and vigor she had for life; the faith in her Savior; the love she had for Pierre, and, at long last, for herself.

Shortly after Paulette's wedding, I received a letter from Jacques saying that he was to be paroled within the year. He was not only taking the missionary discussions, but school courses in the prison as well. Maurice was also coming to church and listening to the missionaries—befriended by Aimee, of all people.

The first week in April, Jean-Marc and I were married at our ward house in Paris. A few weeks after our civil marriage, we went to the temple in Switzerland to be sealed for time and all eternity. I was grateful that years earlier, Church policy in Europe had been changed to allow those without access to a temple, but who held recommends at the time of marriage, to be sealed as soon as they could go to the temple instead of waiting a whole year. I was saddened that my parents were unable to attend my temple wedding, but Jean-Marc's family was there in force, including aunts and uncles and many cousins. Even Pierre and Paulette were there, though Paulette could not yet go through the temple.

Before our sealing, Jean-Marc was baptized and endowed in behalf of Antoine. Only then did we go to be sealed for time and all eternity. After the short ceremony, we went hand in hand to the celestial room to sit together before leaving the temple. I glanced at the couch opposite us and noticed with surprise that the man sitting there had a baby in his arms. I looked over at Jean-Marc to see him staring at the same thing.

"He looks like you . . . it's . . . your brother!" he whispered, and I quickly looked again to see Antoine with little Antoinette in his arms. Both seemed happy and content.

Jean-Marc and I turned to each other in amazement, and then glanced back at the couch, but they were gone. "Did you—?" I began, feeling a warm happiness spread through me.

"Yes, I did, Ari! I did!"

Rain beat against the windows in a steady torrent, as it had done for the past few days. I sat by the window, looking out into the February night. Occasionally, lightning shot through the darkness and thunder sounded like a giant screaming in agony, echoing the swelling pain in my body. *I'm happy,* I thought fiercely with joy, even through the terrible, crashing pain.

Indeed, the last ten months had been the happiest of my entire life. There had been no real period of marriage adjustment for Jean-Marc and me; our missions had prepared us well for constant companionship and sharing. Our love had already learned patience and faith; and that, I knew, was half the battle.

Thunder crashed again both outside and within, and with the glow from the lightning, I saw my parents' car. "They're here!" I yelled, gritting my teeth against the contraction that seemed to pulse throughout my entire body.

Jean-Marc helped gather my things and carried them down to the waiting car. We had our own car now, but I had wanted my husband beside me, holding my hand through the contractions instead of fighting the traffic. So I had called my parents the minute I realized that the false labor I'd been having for weeks had finally become real. Besides, this time I wanted my whole family with me.

Four hours later, I gave birth to twins—a girl and a boy. The love that swelled in my heart as I touched and kissed them seemed to equal the fervent emotion I had felt for my first baby, Nette. My happiness knew no bounds. But I knew that I felt the joy of my present life more intensely because of the pain I'd experienced in the past, and it was worth it.

"Uh, I guess I won't be working for you anymore, Father," I said, looking up into his happy face as I lay on the bed with a warm baby cuddled in each arm. Jean-Marc sat beside me, stroking my hair and gazing down at our children with reverence and love, and not just a little awe.

"Well, under the circumstances, I won't require a month's notice," my father said, smiling.

My mother also looked happy. "It's a lot of work, Ariana, having twins, but it's worth it. They'll take care of each other later on." She wiped a tear from her face, and I knew she was thinking about Antoine, but this time the memories were happy. "And I'll be over every day to help, if you want me to."

"I do, Mother, thank you." There was silence as we stared at the babies, so recently come to earth from heaven.

"Just so you don't go on Wednesday at seven," my father said. "Remember, we have an appointment."

"What!" I said, pretending indignation. "What's more important than these two precious babies?" To emphasize my words, I kissed each little forehead and looked up at my father.

"Well, uh, we . . ." I had never known my father to fumble for words, and wondered what could cause such a thing. I waited curiously while he got himself under control. "You see, the other day some young missionaries from your church knocked on our door, and we decided to hear what they have to say. Not," he held up his hands quickly, "because we want to join, but because we feel it's time we understand our daughter and what she believes."

"That's wonderful!" I exclaimed with a silly smile on my face. I suddenly remembered seeing Antoine and Antoinette in the temple on my wedding day. *We'll see our whole family there yet,* I promised them silently. *We have time.*

My eyes moved to the window, where rain was still beating at the panes. But the sight of the falling drops no longer brought sadness and despair to my heart as they once had. They would always remind me of those I had lost, but the emptiness was completely gone. And now I had a new, happy memory to add to the good rainy-day recollections Jean-Marc and I had already made together.

"It's like you promised, Jean-Marc," I said softly, looking up into his sparkling, green-brown eyes. "I think I'm really starting to love the rain."

About the Author

Rachel Ann Nunes is a busy homemaker, student, and Church worker who lists writing as one of her favorite pursuits. She is currently working toward a degree in English at Brigham Young University, and has published several articles and stories. *Ariana: The Making of a Queen* is her first published novel.

In addition to writing and family activities, Rachel enjoys reading, camping, volleyball, softball, and traveling to or reading about foreign countries.

Rachel and her husband, TJ, are the parents of four children. They live in American Fork, Utah, where Rachel teaches Sunday School in her ward.

Rachel welcomes readers' comments and questions. You can write to her at P.O. Box 353, American Fork, Utah 84003-0353.